SEX SEA

by

William King

WILDSIDE PRESS

WANTON ISLE! Bora-Ka was a beachcomber's paradise—Rod Carlson was the only white man for miles, and the dusky-skinned beauties of the tropics knew only one law: his need. Unfetted by modesty, their greatest delight was to please him, and they fed him delicious fruits, bathed him with waves of love, and sheltered him with their warm, possessive bodies until he floated on a sea of bliss. The only thing he lacked was a white woman, and then he got a sin-filled-yacht-load of them—along with a passion-drenched-yacht-load of trouble! White man knowhow introduced civilized orgies on the primitive innocence of his island harem, and turned his island Eden into a hell of sadistic hunger and passion pain. So when the Gods shrieked their vengeance and the typhoon struck like a howling sword, lust ran amok in a holocaust of passion!

1

—————————————

IN THE FANTASTIC, MULTI-COLORED EXPLO-
sion of a Pacific sunset, Carlson sat on the
smooth and unmarred beach of Bora-Ka and
watched the naked girls play in the surf.

Carlson was completely at peace with the world. It
had taken him a long time, ten years of wandering, to
find this peace, but it was, he thought as he lit one of his
carefully hoarded cigarettes, well worth the searching.
Somewhere, he had always known, there must be a place
where time had no meaning, where the world had not

5

reached in with the savage, bitter disciplines of modern living. He had hunted desperately, like a man searching for his salvation; and at last he had found it. If there were such a thing as Heaven, Carlson thought wryly, it must be far inferior to Bora-Ka.

The bodies of the women in the surf rose and fell above the gentle cresting of the waves that slid over the reef. In the yellow, dying light, the bodies glinted bronze. He saw the bob and jut of water-shiny breasts, the rounded curves of multitudes of unmistakably female buttocks. He heard squeals and laughter of the lilting kind uttered in civilization only by very small children, but common to the happy women of Bora-Ka. Carlson sighed and leaned back on the sand, the cigarette tasting indescribably good, not a tense muscle anywhere in his body.

He was a lean, muscle-plied man in his early thirties. The tropic sun had burned him to a bronze almost equivalent to that of the Polynesians of Bora-Ka, but it had turned his brown hair a scorched, light blond color. It had done the same to his beard and his eyebrows, so that nobody would have mistaken him for one of the natives, all of whom had hair so black that it shone almost blue. He was the only white man on the island, which was the largest one of the Bora-Maka atoll. But the people of Bora-Ka had long since forgotten that he was white, despite the blond hair and blue eyes; they considered him as one of their own. Carlson liked that, he too had nearly forgotten his earlier life. To him, life seemed to have begun when he first set foot on Bora-Ka.

The cigarette had burned down and he tossed it away regretfully. If there were any drawback to Bora-Ka at all, it was this: the atoll was so far off the trade lanes that it was a long time between supplies of tobacco.

But that was its advantage, too. There was nothing on Bora-Ka to attract traders and nothing the natives needed from them. Thus Bora-Ka sat in undisturbed isolation, lost in the far reaches of the Pacific, and remained paradise.

Carlson sat up. The women were coming out of the water now, charging naked and unashamed toward him from the surf. As they ran, their breasts bobbed, their hair streamed, and their teeth glinted whitely in happy laughter. Carlson laughed back at them in spite of himself. Three of those women coming toward him were his.

And suddenly, as they reached him, he was overwhelmed by wet, laughing, sunbrowned bodies. Kama, Valu, and Tesai all leaped on him at once. He was immersed in water-cooled flesh as, playfully, they wrestled him around on the sand. Soft thighs, but with a certain strength, fell across his body. Velvety breasts flattened against him and hungry lips nibbled at his face and throat and shoulders, affectionately. His three women loved him, and they were not niggardly about showing it.

Carlson laughed and wrapped one arm around Kama and another about Valu and held them tightly against him, immobilizing them so they could not rough him around. That left Tesai free, and as Carlson lay back on the sand, holding the other two women tightly, Tesai laughed. He could not defend himself and she attacked him mercilessly.

For a moment, Carlson looked into dark, laughing eyes in a smooth, round face. He saw the tip of a pink tongue protrude sensuously between full lips. The other women of Bora-Ka were gathered about, watching the fun, laughing and nudging each other.

Tesai was eighteen. As were all the island girls at that age, she was well-versed in the art of dealing with a man. She knelt above Carlson. Her naked body bent forward; boobs the size of coconuts dangled and swayed, their nipples hardened not only by the touch of sea water, but by the proximity of her man. Kama and Valu tried to twist loose, but Carlson held them tightly, and said harshly, "Stop it, Tesai! That's for the hut."

Tesai laughed. "On Bora-Ka, my husband, it is for the time, and the place is of no concern. When will you learn that?" Then her lips were moving down Carlson's face. They fastened on his mouth. He felt the thrust of her tongue, eager and hungry. The other two women he held writhed against him, squirming, their lips nibbling at his shoulders, their hips deliberately moving in rhythm against him.

They liked to tease him thus. On Bora-Ka, love-making was a thing to be done when and where one felt like it, but Carlson had never completely got over his white man's inhibition against doing it in public, with a gleeful audience cheering him on. The women knew that and took pleasure in causing him discomfiture by trying to inveigle him into forgetting himself and his inhibitions.

Now Tesai's lips left his and moved to his throat. Her hands were caressing his flanks with slow, thought-out, loving lightness. Carlson wore only a pair of shorts; his flesh was naked and vulnerable. Despite himself, he felt tangible desire at the touch of the woman against him and the soft touch of Tesai's lips.

"That's it, Tesai!" Kama laughed. Carlson had long since learned the simple and liquid language of Bora-Ka, and he spoke and understood it idiomatically. "That's it. Show our husband what it means to be married to the women of Bora-Ka." She squirmed against him enthusiastically.

"Damnit, stop, Tesai!" Carlson laughed in English. He did not dare release the other two women, he knew, if he did his trouble would merely triple. Tesai, who understood practically no English, paid no attention at all to his admonition.

Her hands had slipped lower. They were merciless and the single layer of fabric of the shorts was no protection against them. Her lips were tracking over his chest and then moving down his belly; the tip of her tongue warm against his flesh.

Carlson let out a long breath. Suddenly there was no desire in him to resist any more. He lay back and closed his eyes. He felt Tesai touching the buttons on the shorts.

Then all at once, her hands left him and, as he opened his eyes, he saw her raising her head. At the same time, a cry went up from the other women. "Kesa! Kesa! A ship! A ship!"

Carlson let go of Kama and Valu and sat up quickly, in surprise. A ship? The trading schooner was not due for another month.

All the women were staring seaward. Carlson's eyes followed their pointing hands.

A huge white yacht, unable to cross the reef into the lagoon, had appeared like a giant seabird settling on the water. It was dropping anchor a half mile out beyond the first shelf of coral.

Carlson stood up suddenly. He snapped an order at Kama. "Hurry. Go to the village and tell the men." Obediently, all playfulness gone, she scrambled to her feet and soon disappeared through the open growth of palms that lined the beach.

"My husband," Tesai said wonderingly, "what is such a ship doing here at this time?"

Carlson frowned into the dying light. "I don't know," he said slowly. But already a sense of foreboding was beginning to clinch in him. That yacht was the size of a small freighter, it had obviously cost a fortune. It meant white men and civilization. Carlson had no desire to see either touch Bora-Ka.

As he watched, a small boat was put over the side. In the fading light, he saw a ladder lowered and figures descend. Two figures first, men in tropical whites, so far away they were almost blurs. Then three more figures, and Carlson tensed. Even at that distance he could tell that the three who followed the two were white women, and his heart sank. There had not been a white woman on Bora-Ka in the memory of the islanders, and now here came not one, but three. It was hard to tell, so far away, but the three of them looked young. Carlson caught enough glint of flesh to make out that they were very lightly clad.

Sailors, three of them, finished the complement of the boat. Faintly Carlson heard the chatter of a motor as the boat swung away from the yacht and, breaking a white vee at its nose, sped across the reef toward where he stood.

Carlson stood tensely, waiting. When the boat had

half reached them, he snapped further orders to Valu and Tesai. "Go back to the hut. Put on some clothes."

"No, my husband." Valu's full lips pouted. "I want to see the white men and women who are in that boat. I have never seen white women before."

"Damnit, do what I tell you! You'll get plenty of chance to see white men and white women, I'm afraid." He slapped her hard on the rump. She and Tesai squealed and ran to carry out his command. Some of the other women retreated, too. but most of them stood curiously watching. Carlson flicked a glance at their naked figures. The women of Bora-Ka had magnificent bodies, and for the first time he wished that they were more particular about covering them. These were not friendly and law-abiding natives from a neighboring atoll, these were white men. Carlson was very, very much afraid of white men.

There was sound behind him as the boat neared. He turned to see the men of the village appearing through the growth of palms. Like the women, they had the fine bodies of the unspoiled Polynesian, marked here and there with sacred tattoos and cicatrices. They wore loin cloths only and carried sharp *parangs*, knives they had bought from Malayan traders. Halu, headman of the village and the father of Carlson's three wives, strode up to Carlson. Though tall for a man of Bora-Ka, he barely came up to the six-foot white man's cheek, but he was wide through the shoulders and, even at fifty, his muscles were lean and hard and heavy. There was a glint of intelligence in his eyes and a touch of apprehension that matched Carlson's own, as he said: "Who is it, do you think, my son? Is it the French come back?"

"I don't think so," Carlson murmured. Once, years before, the atoll had been under French mandate and, briefly, there had been a French administrator stationed there. He had pulled out during the Second World War. Theoretically the atoll was now under U.S. administration for the United Nations, but insofar as Carlson knew, he himself was the only American ever to visit Bora-Ka since the war. It was a place of no importance except to the people who lived there. The reef made it impossible to use as a naval base; besides, it was too far off the lines of communication. It produced a tiny bit of copra, but this was all absorbed by the traders who touched there every four or five months. As far as the outside world was concerned, the atoll was simply a dead spot in the vast reaches of the Pacific. That was what had drawn Carlson to it. He prayed silently now that this was just a water stop-over on some rich man's cruise. *Please,* he thought, *don't let it be missionaries or anthropologists. Either kind could mix up a place thoroughly.*

The boat came on, limned against the last glowing color of the sunset that turned the sea into molten gold and spread fiery fingers across a limitless sky. The people of Bora-Ka chattered in wonder, excitement, and speculation.

Then the boat had reached the shore. Its engine died and it beached lightly on the sand. The two men in tropical white got out. The sailors and the three women sat where they were. In the last of the light, Carlson could not tell much about the women except that two of them were blonde and that none of them seemed to be wearing very much. He took a step forward to meet the men.

One of them was short and paunchy, his face heavy-jowled and reddened by sun. He was sweating profusely. The other was taller and very handsome. His upper lip was lined by a thin black mustache and his features were cameo perfect; he was not much older than Carlson.

He stepped in front of the shorter man and faced Carlson and said, in the pidgin of the Pacific: "You belong headman?" Then his eyes narrowed. "Hey," he muttered, "you're blond."

"That's right," said Carlson easily and in English.

The handsome man's mouth dropped open slightly; then he grinned. "Hell, an American. Right?"

"Right," said Carlson.

The man named George said nothing. He just looked at Carlson with eyes set deep in his fat face. His eyes raked Carlson up and down. There was both distrust and disapproval in them.

"Ask them what they're doing here," said Halu, in the Bora dialect.

Carlson nodded. "What do you people want?"

Something flickered in the handsome man's eyes. Instead of answering directly, he said: "I'm Lloyd Farley." He thrust out a hand.

Carlson took it automatically. "Roderick Carlson."

Farley pumped the hand with a strong, enthusiastic grip. "Rod, I'm glad to know you. Do you live here?"

Carlson pulled his hand away. "I live here," he said coolly.

"Fine, fine." There was satisfaction in Farley's voice. "That's going to simplify matters immensely." He turned to the short, fat man. "George Marlowe, meet

Rod Carlson."

"I guess you've heard of me, Carlson," George Marlowe said. His touch was limp and brief.

Carlson shook his head. "No, I don't think so. Should I have?"

He thought that Marlowe's face reddened, but in the last ebb of light, he couldn't be sure. Marlowe grunted deep in his throat.

"Maybe it's just as well," Farley said. His eyes looked at the assembled men of Bora-Ka. "Are there gentlemen friendly or hostile?"

The people of Bora-Ka were the friendliest in the world. There was not, in their dialect, even any word for "hate." But Carlson answered equivocally. "That depends," he said, "on why you're here."

"Oh, yes, that. Well, let's say we're just cruising the Pacific and we stopped off at Bora-Ka to say hello." Farley smiled; his teeth were very white.

"In that case," said Carlson, relaxing a little, "you'll find they're very friendly."

"We thought," Farley went on, "that we'd stay a day or two and see what a real tropical atoll looks like." He swung his eyes around. "Very picturesque. Very . . ." For the first time he seemed to see the naked women. His voice trailed off. His eyes raked up and down the nude brown bodies. "Look at that, George," he whispered. "will you look at that?"

George was looking. "Hell," he said, "I like mine white."

With what was obviously an effort, Farley jerked his eyes away. "Yes," he muttered. "Very picturesque. I've seen things like this in the *National Geographic,* but never in person before. Do they really go around like that all the time, Carlson?"

"They've been swimming," Carlson said tautly. He turned away from them and gave the headman, Halu, the gist of the conversation and introduced him to the two men. That throb of apprehension in him was increasing. He disliked Farley and Marlowe immediately and immensely.

"Well," said Farley, "if everybody's friendly, I guess it's safe for the women to come ashore." He turned toward the boat and gestured, and the women climbed out.

Carlson stared at them as they came up. All the women were in their early twenties. The two blondes were striking. There was a distinct family resemblance. They both had heads of shimmering golden hair that drew breaths of admiration from the staring women of Bora; their eyes were a peculiar dark purple, their lips full and red. They wore matching bras of white, barely concealing four breasts that were mates, full and pushing hard against the restraint of the material. Their shorts were cut low at the hips and high at the thighs, and their legs were long, tanned, and perfect. Obviously sisters, perhaps even twins, they were both very beautiful.

"Anne and Joyce Marlowe," Farley introduced them; "this is Rod Carlson. Anne and Joyce are George's daughters."

"I see," Carlson murmured. He said some conventional thing to them. They nodded without speaking, but he was very much aware of those great purple eyes fastened on him. He was aware that their gazes moved up and down his muscular, sunburned frame with unfeigned admiration.

The third woman moved forward a little impatiently. Carlson, tearing his eyes away from the two blonde
sisters, looked at her and then, involuntarily, sucked in
a breath of admiration.

Her hair was as dark as any Bora maiden's. Blue-
black, it was piled high on her head. Her skin was very
pale, and her eyes were a slumberous black that matched
her hair. Her nose was not tilted like those of the sisters,
but straight and patrician. Her mouth was a crimson
fullness in a firm-chinned face. Her neck was long and
shapely, her shoulders without freckle of blemish, bared
by a low-cut blouse. Carlson gaped at the breasts whose
upper slopes reared themselves above the neckline, whose
points probed at the fabric beneath which there was obviously nothing but woman. The breasts were the largest
he had ever seen — fantastic — yet they stood out
straight and firm without support.

The shorts she wore were longer and less daringly
cut than those of the Marlowe girls, and her legs were
not as heavy; they were long and slender and perfect in
a thoroughbred way, depending on symmetry and not
volume of flesh for their breathtaking beauty. Her dark
eyes fastened directly on Carlson's own, and she said,
without waiting to be introduced, "I'm Margo Neal."

For a moment Carlson's mouth was too dry to answer. It had been five years since he had seen a white
woman. Now, the sight of these three, lovely and nearly
nude themselves, hit him with unexpected impact. He
felt a quick stirring in his legs. There was a new, strange
fire in his veins. He tried hard to show no sign of it,
but he could not help letting his eyes travel boldly over
Margo Neal, and, during that stretched-out second, she

stood quite still and straight, as if inviting his inspection.

Farley coughed. "Margo," he said, "is Mr. Marlowe's fiancée."

"Oh." Carlson came back to reality. He looked from the lovely girl to the squat, fat figure of George Marlowe and he had an immediate and vivid mental picture of the two of them making love — the beautiful woman and the toadlike man. It sickened him oddly.

"It's too dark tonight to see the island," Farley went on, "but perhaps you could tell us something about it. Would you care to join us on the yacht for dinner?"

"I'm afraid I couldn't," Carlson said obstinately.

Margo Neal moved a step closer to him. "Please," she said, and her voice was low and throaty. "We've never met a genuine beachcomber before. It's quite fascinating."

In the darkness, Carlson could catch a faint breath of perfume, sensuous and stirring; like the fragrance of the flowers that his wives liked to wear in their hair. Again that unexpected throb of desire went through him.

His own voice sounded like a stranger's to him as he said slowly: "All right..."

He turned to Halu. "I'm going out to the yacht to talk to them," he said. "They may want more than they've told us. I shall try to find out."

Poker-faced Halu nodded. He put a hand on Carlson's arm. "You have our confidence," he said, and he squeezed. "You are one of us. Do not forget that on the white man's ship."

"Don't worry," Carlson said. "I won't." He turned and looked through the darkness. Someone had lighted a torch. In its flickering glare, he saw his three women standing back from the group modestly, their faces both curious and a little frightened at their first sight of white women.

He walked over to them. "It is necessary for me to go to the ship of the white men. I shall be late tonight returning. Eat your fish and taro without me."

Disappointment showed in the faces of all three. And Tesai stepped forward and took his arm. "Please, our husband," she said, "you will not go off with the white men? You will not leave us?"

Carlson laughed and patted her shoulder. "Never," he said to the three of them. "I shall stay here until fish grow legs and climb trees." It was the Bora way of saying always, and he was pleased at the diminuation of fear that showed on the three faces. When a man had said it, it was so — that was the way of the people of Bora.

Carlson turned back to the white men. "All right," he said. "Let's go."

Margo Neal was looking at him intently. As they walked toward the boat, she asked: "All three of those women are yours?"

"Yes," said Carlson tersely. "It's the way of Bora."

He heard her draw in a deep breath. Her voice was very soft and husky. "You must be quite a man," she said.

2 ━━━━━━━━━━━━━━━━━━━━━━━━━

BOARDING THE YACHT WAS LIKE REENTER-
ing a world he had long since forgotten. It
was a world of rich fabrics and shining furniture and enclosed spaces and artificial light-
ing, a world as different from that of Bora-Ka as day
from night. The dining saloon of the yacht was large,
paneled with rich woods. Naked except for his shorts,
Carlson felt out of place for the first time in years.

"We have some very good Scotch," Farley told him.
A Filipino messboy hovered nearby, attentively. Carlson

licked his lips. Scotch! He'd not tasted Scotch since —
hell, it was so long he couldn't remember. For him on
Bora-Ka there had only been the mild native wine made
from fermented coconut, or an occasional drink of some
raw blend with a trader.

"That would be fine," he said, trying hard to keep a
tremor of anticipation out of his voice. "On the rocks,
please." In a moment they were seated in chairs around
a table and Carlson had a glass in his hand. He enjoyed
the aroma of it first, tantalizing himself with the smoky
effluvium that rose from it like a mist. Then he allowed
himself a taste, and then another taste.

"Drink up," Farley said heartily. "There's plenty
more. What would you like for dinner tonight?"

The Scotch made a warm burn in his stomach. *I
must go slow*, he cautioned himself, *I'm out of practice*.
"steak," he heard himself say. "Do you by any chance
have any steak?"

"There's a reefer full of aged sirloin," Farley murmured.

"God," Carlson whispered to himself, hunger gouging at him. The staple of Bora-Ka's diet was fish. The
ocean yielded an infinite variety -- but after several
years, fish was only fish. You ate it to keep alive, for no
other reason. There had been times when Carlson would
lie awake at night and dream of the solid texture of a
good steak between his teeth. "Steak and potatoes," he
said. "Just plain old steak and potatoes. Very rare ..."

The whiskey was getting to him a trifle. He told
himself not to gulp the rest of it in his glass, but he
did and, before it was truly gone, Farley was refilling it
for him. Carlson looked around the table. The gimbal

light overhead was striking gleams from the white hillocks of the bosoms of the women; the blondes with their tight bras squeezing their breasts together and thrusting them upward, Margo Neal leaning forward and looking at him intently, the neckline of the blouse sagging forward, the lovely curved flesh of those firm mounds visible nearly to the nipples . . . Suddenly it was good. It was good — just for this little while — to be sitting on a real chair at a real table drinking real whiskey, waiting for a real steak and looking at real American girls.

Margo Neal asked quietly, "Mr. Carlson, I'm curious. What are you doing on Bora-Ka?"

Suddenly it all vanished. All at once he saw it for the trap it was, and he drove the pleasure of it out of his mind with memories of the freedom and unspoiled peace of the atoll. "Let's just say," he murmured, setting down his glass, "that I'm a fugitive from the rat race."

"What are you?" Marlowe rumbled. "Some kinda beatnik? Suddenly his heavy jowels split. He had bad teeth, and they showed in his thick-lipped grin. "Or is it beachnik?" He laughed phlegmily and inordinately.

"Daddy," one of the Marlowe girls said reproachfully. Carlson thought it was Joyce, he was not sure. They were so much alike that he'd lost track of which was which.

"Please," Margo Neal urged. "Please, I'm very curious to know."

Carlson sighed. He did not like to think about it, but there was really no harm in telling them. Probably they would not understand anyhow.

"I've been out here five years," he said, staring into his glass. "Back in the States, I used to be with Holden,

Fynch, McLean, and Whippet."

Marlowe looked interested. "The advertising agency?"

"That's right. I was an account executive. Did you ever hear of Nonoffend, Mr. Marlowe?"

"Hell, yes. The deodorant made by Fliegel Cosmetics. I just bought a controlling interest in that outfit last year."

Carlson nodded. "All right. I was married. I was earning fourteen thousand a year, with a lock on twenty in a couple more years and a damn nice Christmas bonus. And all I had to do for it was map out the campaigns for Nonoffend and sell them to the manufacturer. Armpits." His voice turned suddenly bitter. "I became a specialist in armpits, Mr. Marlowe."

One of the Marlowe girls giggled.

"Yeah," Carlson said. "It sounds hilarious. Until it actually becomes the work you have to do. Until it becomes the paramount concern of your life. You go to school," he said. "You go to school and you study, you get a liberal arts education, you study Greek drama and the Elizabethan theatre and modern English and American literature and you grow up wanting to do something with words. But you get married to a girl whose old man is president of an advertising agency, and suddenly you find that all you can do with words is write about armpits. And it's fine for a while, but one day you suddenly think: What the hell? What kind of work is this for a grown man to be doing? And you think, there must be something else in the world besides armpits. You want to go and find out. You've read and dreamed of all the marvelous places in the world and the wonderful people, and the way they live and work and play and, yes, smell ... And you feel life dribbling away between your fingers like sand. You live in a house in the suburbs and you commute and you drink too much and you play footsie with other men's wives and there's always something going on and there's never any time to stop and think about anything, and you wake up in the middle of the night wondering, what else is there to say about armpits? So you try to persuade your wife. You try to persuade the people who are conscious of their armpits, that they are only part of the body, not, a way of life, where there's sunshine and blue water and clean shore . . . But that's not what she wants. What she wants is for you to work along with Daddy and be a nice boy and become very big in armpits. And one thing leads to another and you wind up divorced and you tell the old man to take his job and ram it, and she's a witch and she strikes at you for more alimony than you could ever pay, and you just take off. You take off for Tahiti, because you've always heard that it's a paradise on earth and it's where people run to. But Tahiti turns out to be just another tourist trap and a lot of the people there are very conscious of their armpits, and it's not what you're looking for at all. So you get a job on a trading schooner, and you beat around the Pacific for a while, and one day you call in at Bora-Ka, the minute you see it you know this is it." He let out a long breath, "Sure, it sounds absurd. But that's the way it was with me, absurd or not."

Margo Neal said, "I don't think it's absurd. I think it was very courageous."

Farley was staring at Carlson. "So you've been to Tahiti, eh? And you found it a big disappointment."

"That's right. Oh, hell, it's all right for tourists. It's a nice place to visit, but I wouldn't want to live there."

"No," said Farley, "no, of course not. We've been to Tahiti too, and we know exactly what you mean."

Carlson sipped the last of his second drink. His head was buzzing slightly, and he knew he'd better not have the third. But he made no protest when Farley poured more whiskey into his glass. Carlson patted his pocket. "You wouldn't have a cigarette, would you?"

"Get Mr. Carlson a couple of cartons," Farley said to the Filipino. His dark eyes stayed fastened on Carlson. "So you've found paradise here on Bora-Ka."

"Pretty close to it," said Carlson.

"Well, the natives are Polynesians, as you saw. Pure Polynesian, something very hard to find these days. But Bora-Ka's always been so far off the shipping lanes, has no tactical or strategic value. It's been let alone and the blood has never mixed. There are about two hundred people on the island, roughly three women to every man. Living's easy if you don't want too much; fish practically jump out of the sea, coconuts drop in your lap, there's a taro and a kind of plantain. It's never too cold, never too hot. There's a good deal of rain, but there's plenty of sunshine, too. There are no animals on the island at all, not even rats, and except for a few landcrabs who live in the coconut groves, no other pests."

"What about the people?"

"They're a very unusual sort of people," Carlson said with great sincerity. "First of all, isolated as they are, the tradition of war and killing has vanished from the society. They find it inconceivable that one man could take the life of another. Killing is what you do to fish, not to men. They're very peaceable, although I suppose they could be fighters if there were sufficient reason. They drink very little, only a mild coconut wine. They practice polygamy because of the surplus of women. It's mandatory for every male to have at least three wives. The women long ago discovered some kind of root that grows on the island that limits conception, and they drink a tea made from it regularly. I suppose it contains some sort of steroid or other hormone; I don't know. Thus they're able to control the population, never get overcrowded and suffer from the friction that overcrowding leads to. There are no sexual taboos on Bora-Ka. If a man's wives prove insufficient for him, which is unlikely, he can always borrow the wife or wives of a friend to lend variety. To the people of Bora-Ka, the act of sex is like the act of eating, it can be performed either publicly or privately, with no particular shame one way or the other."

"It does sound like paradise," Margo Neal murmured.

Carlson allowed himself a fleeting smile.

"So, it's a place where there's no hate, no covetousness, no hunger, and no sexual dissatisfaction. Consequently, there is no neurosis and there are no psychosis. If a deformed child is born, which is very rare, it is loved and treated and cared for exactly as if it were perfect. When it grows up, it may marry, but it may not reproduce, which can be controlled by the tea the women drink. Consequently, defective strains of all kind, mental and physical, have just about bred out of existence."

"Wonderful," Farley said. "It sounds like Huxley's *Brave New World* without the horror."

"No," said Carlson, "it's a very old world. It's perhap. the way the world was before Eve ate the apple, before Cain slew Abel. It has nothing to do with the New World at all. And if I have my way, it never will." Suddenly caution touched him. "Why are your people so interested in Bora-Ka?"

Farley shrugged. "Who wouldn't be interested in paradise?"

Carlson looked around the lushly funished saloon. "I don't think it would be your cup of tea," he said thinly. "I don't think it would be your cup of tea at all."

"Probably not," said Farley. "Certainly not for a long time, the way you've had it. Come, let's have another drink. The steaks should be along soon."

Too much Scotch. The rest of the evening blurred for Carlson. Marlowe stayed in the background, drinking heavily. Farley, Carson knew, was pumping him, but it had been so long since he had talked in English to an intelligent American ...

And the women. Like it or not, he could not keep his eyes off them. The two Marlowe girls were poems of blonde voluptuousness, but it was Margo Neal to whom he was really drawn. He could sense in her an intensity, a depth of passion, smoldering fires, that were totally unlike the easy-going, simple placidity of the island women. It had been a long time since he had been around a woman like her.

"You'll spend the night with us, of course," Farley said much later in the evening.

"Oh, no. My wives are waiting for me."

Farley chuckled. "So a man's the slave of his wives

even on Bora-Ka, eh?"

"No," Carlson heard himself say indignantly. "On Bora-Ka, there's no questioning of what the man chooses to do."

"Then why worry about your wives? How long has it been since you've slept on a real mattress? What do you sleep on there on the island. Reed matting?"

"Yes," Carlson said.

"And a wooden pillow, I'll bet."

Carlson nodded.

"Spend the night in a real bed again," Farley said. "Eat a civilized breakfast with us. We'll be happy to run you back to the island in the morning."

Carlson looked at Marlowe. The fat man, who had drunk more than all the rest in the room combined, was slumped down in his chair. He was nearly asleep, his stertorous breath making thick lips flutter.

"He won't mind?" said Carlson thickly. The thought of a real bed was tempting.

"Have some more Scotch," said Farley. "Of course he won't mind."

"All right," Carlson heard himself say, against his better judgment. "All right, if you'll make sure I get back to the island right after breakfast."

"Of course," Lloyd Farley said smoothly.

Carlson lay in darkness in a private stateroom, his body enjoying the luxury of the mattress and pillow, his head still floating from all the Scotch. Outside, he was aware of the gentle, muted sound of the ocean lapping at the yacht's hull. He wondered what time it was. It was the first time in years that he had ever needed to do that. His wrist watch had long since ceased to work and had been discarded. Tesai, as the oldest of the three sisters and his senior wife, wore it around her neck on a string of cowrie shells.

It was very dark in the stateroom. Carlson had the odd sensation of being in a trap. This was the first time in a long while that he had slept where fresh air and ocean breezes could not freely cross his body.

He stirred restlessly, the mattress was too soft. Or was it that? Was it more than that? Was it a worm planted within him by this civilized evening — the whiskey and the steak and the women? Most of all, the women. He remembered the shadowy cleft between Margo Neal's breasts, the slumberous dark beauty of her eyes, speaking of tensions and delights of which Tesai, Valu, and Kama had never dreamed.

She was Marlowe's mistress, of course. But beyond that, what was she? Carlson rubbed his hand over his eyes, unable to get her out of his mind.

He did not know how long he lay and tossed before there was, in the darkness, a minute fraction of sound. It was close at hand, and suddenly he realized that his door had opened.

He sat up quickly. "Who is it?" His fingers groped for the light switch, but he could not find it.

"Shh," a voice said. "It's Margo." The voice was a barely audible whisper in the darkness, and he heard the door close.

Something jumped inside Carlson like a shark leaping out of the water after a flying fish. His whisper matched her own. "What do you want?" His groping fingers found a switch over the bed, a tiny reading light flicked on.

Carlson stared at her.

She stood before him clad only in a negligee that was absolutely transparent. The thin, exciting folds of the garment flowed over those fantastically large breasts, which still stood proudly forward without support, and he saw that her nipples were large and pink, not brown, and that their centers were hard and jutting. His eyes traveled down the rest of her body, plainly revealed in the light. He saw the narrow waist, the rounded plane of the belly, the magnificent legs. His heart hammered wildly. She was so different, so entirely different, from the women of Bora-Ka.

Her eyes were half-lidded. It was almost as if she herself were in some kind of trance. He saw the tip of her tongue run over one red lip. "What do I want?" she whispered. "What do you think I want?"

Suddenly Carlson realized that, having taken off his shorts, he was even more naked than she. Her eyes were running up and down his muscle-plied body hungrily. Carlson stood up, long since past shame.

"Where's Marlowe?" he whispered. "I thought —"

Her lip curled. "Marlowe's dead drunk, asleep. The way he is nearly every night, the fat —" Her voice throbbed with contempt. Suddenly she moved toward him and her voice was urgent. "Carlson," she said almost frantically, and then the negligee dropped and she was in his arms.

He felt the long, velvety length of her, warm and vital, against him, lips already in motion, breasts flattening their soft weight against his chest, nipples gouging at him. Her mouth was a dark, hungry, red-rimmed hole in which the tongue flickered like an imprisoned snake. Her eyes closed. He kissed her, kissed her hard, and she surged against him, mouth opening wide, tongue long and desperate.

He felt the shock wave of her. His hand traveled down her smooth back, touched one fine, rounded buttock. She pushed against him, and Carlson sank back to the bed while they were still locked together in that embrace.

Carlson's hands found her breasts and Margo moaned, her eyes tightly closed. Carlson caressed them, his thumbs moving across the nipples. Margo's breath was a series of explosions into his mouth, her thigh against him as she moved her body.

Carlson could wait for no more foreplay, and apparently neither could she. He still held her breasts as she rolled over on her back. Her legs moved to gather him in. His lips tore away from hers and went to the nipples of her breasts, first one and then the other. He kissed the warmth of them as Margo pulled him down, brooking no further delay.

She was incredibly delightful. It was as if her body had a life of its own. It did things to Carlson, drew him inward, forced him outward, pulled him back inward again.

Carlson felt himself becoming a blur. His face was buried in her breasts, his nostrils full of her perfumed fragrance. She was muttering something over and over in explosive syllables he could catch little of. He heard her say: "That's it. That's it. Oooh . . ." Her body convulsed, every muscle spasming, and then it started all over again.

That happened to her three times before it happened to Carlson. She had been a bomb waiting to be triggered into explosion, and that was what she did — she almost literally exploded. Carlson felt himself reaching a pinnacle that was excruciating. Then he shuddered into slow relief.

At last, exhausted for the moment, he sank down on the warmth beneath him that was Margo Neal. She lay inertly, as if she had no strength left.

But as moments passed, and they were still locked together, with not a word going between them, only the steady rasp of their breathing filling the room, he felt Margo coming alive beneath him again. First in little rippling, invitational, tentative spasms, then in a more forthright stirring of her body. Her buttocks began to shift again.

Her new life transmitted itself to Carlson. He felt the rebirth of strength and desire. All at once it seemed to him that he could never get enough of this delicious white woman. It had been so long, so damned long, and Kittie, his wife, had never been very good in bed anyhow ... Margo Neal was, for him, a totally new experience; a white woman who really knew how to make love.

But when it was finished the second time for Carlson, they were both thoroughly satiated. At last he rolled aside, and after a moment he sat up and found his cigarettes and lit two and handed Margo one.

"This," he said, "was an unexpected pleasure."

"Yes." She stood up, reached for her negligee, and shrugged into it. "For me, too."

"Marlowe. You're his mistress?"

"I'm his mistress," she said. Her mouth tautened.

"You're not the only one who has been caught up in something," she said. "A bed can be a trap, too."

"Why do you stay with him?"

"He's a repulsive creature. But he has money. I get some of it. Someday I'll marry him and get a lot more of it."

"And that's what you want?"

"What else is there to want?" Margo said. Her face softened. "Except what you just gave me."

"Then you shouldn't have come here. Suppose he finds out?"

"He won't find out. He's dead drunk. He's always dead drunk at night."

"Marlowe's rich, isn't he?"

She nodded. "Very much so. Filthily so."

"What's he in?"

She shrugged. "I don't know. Big city real estate, various industries, the stock market — I don't know. Everything, I guess."

"Those two girls. Are they really his daughters?"

He thought her eyes clouded for an instant. "They're his daughters. They're also a couple of little —" She characterized them with an unprintable word. "They take after their father," she said tautly.

"And Farley? Who's he?"

"Farley? Farley's an idea man. A promoter. A buzzard who hangs around rich men — and rich men's daughters."

Carlson ground out his cigarette and asked the question he had really been leading up to. "And what do they want here?"

Margo Neal's eyes locked with his. "They'll have

to tell you that."

"Is that all you can say?"

She looked away from him. "It's all I can say. Except ... except for one thing."

"What's that?"

Margo Neal turned toward the door.

"Don't let them touch your island," she said. "They ruin everything they get their hands on." She halted at the door, her face softening. "I can sleep tonight," she said. "For the first time in a long while. Thank you. I don't meet many *men* in my business. Good night." Then she had faded, simply vanished silently through the door like a ghost dissolving in mist.

The door closed behind her. Carlson lit another cigarette and stood rigidly for a long moment staring at it, lost in thought.

3

WHILE A SEAMAN STOOD BY THE RAIL WITH
a shot gun loaded with rifled slugs in case of
sharks, Anne and Joyce Marlowe swam in
the blue water alongside the yacht.

Unlike the girls of Bora-Ka, they did not swim in
the nude. Their bodies would have been less exciting,
thought Carlson, watching them, if they had. What they
wore emphasized, rather than covered, their primary
and secondary sexual characteristics. As they climbed
dripping up the ladder after the swim, the bras of their

bikinis were merely little patches over the ends of their breasts, the taut nipples visible through the fabric; the lower halves of their bikinis were hardly more than g-strings. To Carlson, accustomed to watching women swim naked, there was almost something obscene about the emphasis the bathing suits laid on the crucial parts of their bodies.

They climbed over the rail and stood dripping on the deck as another seaman handed them towels. They were not twins, Carlson had learned, despite their nearly identical appearance. Joyce was a full year older than Anne.

Their violet eyes wandered over Carlson, and he felt the intensity of their gazes. They were, he thought, very much like two hungry animals. You could almost sense the hunger in them. They made no secret of it, did nothing to hide it.

Carlson turned away, and as he did so, he caught sight of an outrigger canoe coming toward the yacht over the reef. In the prow of it sat Halu, the headman, his father-in-law, arms folded. A crew of six men plied the paddles which drove the long canoe forward.

Carlson smiled. Halu had probably been worried about him. So also would have been Tesai, Kama, and Valu. Probably they had driven their father into making the voyage out here to check up on him.

"Hooaa," Halu wound the long note on a shell horn as the canoe approached. It brought Marlowe's daughters around.

"Look," Joyce said. "Look at that. The native men."

There was a throbbing undertone in Anne's voice. "Aren't they gorgeous?"

"They're gassers," Joyce murmured. "Real gassers. Look at those muscles."

Carlson saw Anne lick her lips. "I hope we stay here a while," she whispered.

Carlson stepped forward. "Listen, girls."

They turned and looked at him curiously. Their blonde hair, released from bathing caps, glittered and shimmered in the morning sun.

"Listen, don't go getting any ideas about the men of Bora-Ka." Carlson's voice was stern.

"Why not?" Joyce's voice was a little angry, a trifle defiant. "We've never seen men like that before."

"They're gorgeous," Anne said again.

"They're from another world," Carlson's words rapped at them harshly. "It's not your world at all. You stay clear of them."

Joyce's eyes slitted. "Oh? Well, you and their women seem to have matched up worlds all right."

"That's because I'm in their world, I've accepted it. Their world's fine the way it is. They've got everything they want and they want everything they've got. Don't go building new wants in them."

Joyce was about to reply when Margo Neal came on deck. She looked at Carlson briefly and expressionlessly and at the two girls with dislike. Farley emerged from the companionway behind her. His smile was oily as he said good morning to Carlson, and then he saw the canoe. "What's this? A formal visitation?"

"You might call it that," Carlson murmured.

"Fine." Farley snapped an order at a seaman. "Go get some presents for them. Do they smoke?" he asked Carlson.

"No," Carlson said. "They like cloth, though. Cloth's hard to come by."

"Get a couple of bolts of that madras," Farley snapped. "And a box of jewelry."

Carlson frowned. "Do you usually carry trade goods?"

"They always come in handy," Farley said smoothly. "When they come on board, Carlson, tell them how honored we are by their visit. Ask them to be our guests for breakfast."

"They had breakfast an hour ago," Carlson said.

The canoe had come alongside. In a moment, Halu appeared over the rail. At the sight of Carlson, his face beamed with relief. "My son," he said in the dialect. "Your wives were worried about you."

"I could not refuse the hospitality of the ship," Carlson said. "I was just about to return."

Halu's eyes took in the two blonde girls standing intently watching the Bora men climb aboard. "Hai," he said, "The yellow-haired girls have eyes for our men. They are fine looking women. I would like to borrow one of them myself for a night."

"I don't think it can be arranged," Carlson said, still in the dialect. "Americans do not lend their women."

"Americans have no courtesy, then," said Halu. "We will be happy to lend the Americans our women. We have come to invite them to a *lamua*, a feast tonight."

"I do not think that advisable," Carlson said.

Halu frowned. "But it is the custom. Always, when strangers come." He looked much distressed. The men of Bora put much emphasis on the courtesies of living.

Carlson sighed. Even if Margo had not given him

that cryptic warning last night, he would not have wanted
the people from the yacht ashore. They were intruders,
and instinctively he was afraid of them.

But he could not make an issue of it with Halu.
There were no terms in which he could explain to Halu
that all people were not necessarily as straightforward
and full of good will as the people of Bora. He said, reluctantly, "We shall see. The white people are honored
by your visit, they say, and they have presents for you."

"All the more reason," said Halu, "why they must
be given a *lamua.*"

Carlson sighed. "Oh, very well," he said.

An hour later, they were ready to depart for the
island. The six men of Bora had dispersed, wandering in
admiration and wonder about the yacht, to look at everything on it. Halu had received the presents and had
drunk coffee, not entirely sure that he liked it, while
Carlson ate a breakfast of bacon and eggs. Farley kept
up a running flow of courtesies and florid protestations
of good will to Halu through Carlson, giving Carlson no
time to talk about anything else. Margo Neal was silent
through the meal, and the two Marlowe sisters, who had
already eaten, were not present.

At last, at Halu's insistence, Carlson tendered the
invitation to the *lamua.*

"*Lamua?* What's that?" asked Farley, his handsome face interested.

"A sort of a feast and a dance in your honor. There'll
be cooked fish and taro and plantain and coconut wine
and ceremonial dancing."

"It sounds very interesting," said Farley. "Would it

liven things up any if I brought along a case of gin?"

Carlson half rose, suddenly angry. "Look, these people drink almost nothing. You leave your gin on the boat —"

Farley's grin was placatory. "It was just an offer. Don't you see how you can have a decent party without something to get soused on."

"We manage," Carlson said coldly.

Farley shrugged. "Okay, you're the boss."

"I think we'd better go now," said Carlson to Halu. "My wives are waiting."

As they went up the companionway, topside, Carlson's eyes flicked back to Margo Neal very briefly. She looked at him without expression for a moment, and then her eyes dropped to her plate.

Tekua, the son of Remaua, was the strongest paddler in the entire village and the best man on the water. He was tall and wide-shouldered, and, at the age of nineteen, his muscles were symmetrically perfect and hard as iron.

Tekua had never been on a ship like this before. Neither had any of his mates. They drifted apart, wandering around the ship, wide-eyed with wonder at what they saw. Surely, thought Tekua, the white men must strain to paddle such enormous canoes. What had engaged his interest were the motor-lifeboats that sat in canvas-covered splendor amidships.

Tekua plucked at the edge of the lashed-down canvas, anxious to see what was in the boat. Perhaps there was a store of coconuts, the emergency rations the men of Bora carried when they made a long sea voyage. Or would there be dried fish? He worked the knot loose deftly and lifted the corner of the canvas and gasped at the size of the boat.

"Do you like it?" a voice said incomprehensibly in English at his elbow. It was a woman's voice. The voice of Joyce Marlowe, though Tekua had no idea of her name or what she said.

He smiled at her, showing perfect white teeth. His eyes roved over the full breasts, hidden by patches of cloth at the ends, down the amazingly white belly. He wondered why she wore the little square of cloth between her thighs? Was there something there she was ashamed of?

Ai, he doubted it. She was a fine-looking woman. He wondered if the whites would lend her to him for a few moments. She would be interesting to try out.

"What man speaks for you?" he asked her in his own dialect. Courtesy demanded that the woman's man first give his permission. Every woman had either husband, father or brother to speak for her, and it was very bad taste, in fact unthinkable, to take a woman without asking for her, even for just a little while. It was like borrowing another's fish net without obtaining permission.

Joyce shrugged and gave him a smile. "I don't know what you said, buster," she murmured, "but I like the way you say it." She put out a hand and let it run over the satiny skin that encased iron-hard muscles.

Tekua frowned. It was not wise or seemly for her to do that before he'd obtained permission. As her hand moved away from his arm to his abdomen and stroked the hard, ridged muscles there, he thought about backing away. But the white *vahine* had such soft palms. One would think she had never touched a fish net or a reed bundle for weaving into mats in her life. He stood still, enjoying the circular caress of her palm.

Then the woman was moving very close to him. The little bits of cloth that covered the ends of her breasts were jammed against him. Tekua felt a rush of blood through his body, and he responded instantly to her presence. His fingers impatiently yanked away the bits of cloth that covered her nipples; his hands tested the weight and softness of her startling white breasts. They were good, very good.

And when he did that, something surprising happened to the white girl. She seemed to become very nervous. Her eyes glittered, her lips parted, she moved her body against Tekua. Tekua wished he could make her understand. . .

But she would not wait for any more explanations. She pointed commandingly to the lifeboat, and then she swung lithely into it. Tekua hesitated, wondering if he should follow. Then he heard the girl's impatient voice: "For God's sake, come on." He did not know the words, but he recognized the urgency in the tone very well. Tekua had been active since he was thirteen.

Well, this was no time for worrying about the proprieties. It must be that the white women did things in a different way. It would have been so much simpler out here on the deck, why did she have to climb into the boat? Still—Tekua shrugged, and climbed easily into the boat, disappearing beneath the canvas.

Once inside, he gasped with surprise. Ai, no wonder she wore that piece of cloth at her thighs. She had removed it and it gave him momentary pause. Then her hands and lips were at him. She pushed Tekua back, and she attacked him like a shark attacking a swimmer. She came at his belly, but not with her teeth, with her lips. Her mouth was suddenly all over Tekua; all right, this was part of the Bora-Ka lovemaking. But in the name of the supreme *aku,* what was she doing now? She had loosed his loin cloth, and now — Tekua went rigid. Nobody on the island of Bora-Ka had ever dreamed of such a thing. Nobody would believe him when he told them what the white women did.

He was shocked to the very depths of his soul. But what she was doing also brought every nerve completely alive in him, and he lacked the will power to protest. Besides, he was a man of courtesy, and if this was the way of the white woman, it was not polite to deride it.

But he was relieved when she raised her head. Her eyes glittered at him, and she put her hands on his shoulders and went over backward, pulling him down to her

Tekua let out a breath of relief. This he could understand. And the white woman smelled good, very good, and she felt good, and, ai! her legs were like soft iron around him. . .

At the very moment when she clawed and tensed at the pinnacle of ecstasy, he heard his name called. "Tekua! Where in the name of the Wind God are you?" It was Halu and he was very irritated.

Just in time, Tekua thought, smiling. Politely, he said, "Thank you very much," and disengaged himself from the woman and slithered out from under the canvas.

"Hey," Joyce yelled, twisting and turning in the bottom of the boat. "Hey, damn you, come back! Come back."

But Tekua hastened on. It was not comfortable to

suffer Halu's displeasure, he had a tongue like a knife. Besides, Tekua had a thing of surpassing amazement to tell the others.

Carlson's three women were waiting for him at the village. Naked to the waist, they sat in the sunshine before the thatched hut that was open to the sea on one side, and speculated.

"Did you see the whiteness of those women?" Kama asked.

"They were very white and very beautiful," Tesai said morosely. "Did you see the two who had hair like the sunrise over the sea?"

"Like our husband's hair," said Valu.

"They were very like our husband in many ways," Kama said. "I wonder if he borrowed one of them for the night."

"I do not know," said Tesai. "If he did, I hope she was not very good."

"The white woman he had before was not very good," said Valu. "He told us about her, remember? She lay like a stick on her mat and she wanted him to do all the work."

"Let us hope all white women are the same," said Tesai. "Our husband must not become discontented with us. For it is true that we are not of his own kind and he is not of ours."

"He is almost of ours," Valu said.

"He has worked hard to become one of us," said Tesai. "But always there is that difference in him that, like his sun-colored hair, sets him apart. There is a restlessness in him which our men do not know. An impatience."

"We must make sure that when he compares us to the white woman," said Kama firmly, "we do not come off second best. Whose turn is it with him tonight, my sisters?"

"It is my turn," said Valu. "But I will give him up to Tesai. Tesai is much better than I am."

"Don't be ridiculous," Tesai said. "I am no better than you or Valu."

Unselfishly, the three girls argued among themselves. Each courteously advanced some reason why the other was found more attractive by Carlson. At last Tesai made an impatient gesture.

"Enough of this bickering," she said. "When our husband comes home, we must not wait until night." She tensed. "Look, here come the men from the canoe now."

"But our husband is not with them," said Valu. "Hai, Tekua, where is Carlson?"

Tekua paused and smiled down at them. "He is at the hut of your father in conference. He said to tell you he will be along in the passage of a very short time."

"Did you go aboard the white ship?" Tesai asked.

Tekua laughed. "That I did." He squatted down. "And you would never believe what happened."

"Tell us."

Tekua told them in great detail about his encounter with the yellow-haired white woman.

The eyes of all three girls widened in amazement. "You're joking," Tesai said.

"I am not joking," Tekua insisted. "She did that to me."

"With her lips?"

"With her lips."

Valu shook her head in amazement.

"Who ever heard of such a thing?"

Tekua shrugged. "It is the way of the white woman," he said with infinite worldliness, and then he got up and walked away.

The three girls looked at each other.

"Our husband has never mentioned that," said Kama.

"Nor has he asked us to perform it," Tesai said.

"But it is the way of the white woman," said Valu. "You heard Tekua."

Tesai took a deep breath and looked doubtful.

"So it must be our way, too," said Kama. "We must not allow our husband to grow restless."

Valu nodded. Tesai looked thoughtful. At last, she giggled and shrugged.

Carlson left the hut of Halu and walked toward his own, head bent and deep in thought. He had tried to warn Halu that the intentions of the people on the yacht were not of the best, but Halu simply could not comprehend how they could do the islanders any harm. For that matter, neither could Carlson, but a nagging doubt would not be still within him.

They had said they would only be here a day or two. And in that time, how much harm could they do? There was nothing on Bora-Ka that they could possibly want. There was nothing here but sea and sand and sun and peace, and Americans were not any more notable for being enamored of peace than any other nation. No, the very tranquility of the place would soon bore them and they would leave.

Somehow the thought both relieved and depressed Carlson. He wanted them to go — but he could not get the thought of Margo Neal out of his mind. And at the thought, it seemed to him that he could feel again the touch of her velvety skin against his and smell the fragrance of her perfume. He wanted the rest to go, but somehow he wanted Margo not to go.

He laughed aloud. "A tart," he said in English. "A rich man's mistress." Calling her names like that made him feel better, and he felt even better still when he reached his own hut and found the girls waiting for him.

He looked at them fondly as he approached. Tesai, with her breasts the size and shape of coconuts; Kama, with smaller, sharp-pointed breasts and a slender waist; the good-natured Valu, whose breasts were less firm than the others but who made up any deficiencies in the upper part with fine expertise in the lower. "Hell," he said aloud, as if trying to convince himself, "I've got everything. What more could a man want?"

Then, with squeals of delight, the girls were running toward him. They all embraced him at once. His face was covered with kisses, and six breast points rubbed against his torso. "Our husband!" Tesai cried. "We are so glad you have returned."

Laughing, Carlson patted her and tried to disengage himself from the three pairs of arms. "Wait a minute, wait a minute."

"Did you borrow a white girl?" asked Kama.

"Was she very good?" Valu threw in the question eagerly.

Carlson hesitated. But there was no stigma attached

to having "borrowed" another woman. A man was away from his own wives overnight and it was the sensible thing to do, from the viewpoint of the islanders. He said at last: "Yes, I borrowed the white woman with the dark hair."

"Was she good?" cried Tesai. "Was she as good as we are?"

"She was very good," Carlson said with involuntary truthfulness.

"Ai," said Valu, pulling him into the hut. "But we shall be better. Let us show you a thing we have learned while you were away, Carlson."

Five minutes later, a shocked Carlson said, "Stop that! Where did you learn that?"

Tesai raised her head and looked at him with huge, dark, hurt eyes.

"You do not like it?"

"Where did you learn it?" Carlson insisted. His face was twisted with a kind of fury.

"Tekua also borrowed a white woman, one of the ones with golden hair, while he was aboard the ship this morning. He said it was the way of the white woman."

"And if it is the way of the white woman," put in Kama plaintively, "it must be our way, too. We do not want you to become restless."

"Did Tekua not tell us true?" asked Tesai.

Carlson took in a deep breath. "He told you true."

"And is it something white men like?"

Carlson did not answer. He was staring out at the yacht, white as a seabird, riding at anchor beyond the reef.

Hell, he thought bitterly, *it's started already.*

"Only if it is something the woman wants to do," he said patiently.

"We always want to do what will make you happy," said Kama.

"You are our husband," said Valu.

Carlson saw that the girls were on the verge of tears. Suddenly he realized that he had spoiled a carefully planned surprise.

"I prefer the island way," he said, and let himself be dragged down by the three pairs of eager arms.

4

IN THE STATEROOM SHE SHARED WITH George Marlowe. Margo Neal sat drinking steadily, though it was only eleven o'clock in the morning.

Carlson... The name kept running over and over through her brain. *Carlson...*

She stared sourly down at her glass. She was drinking too much these days. She told herself that she must cut down. If she didn't, her looks would start to go; if her looks went, everything went.

Clad only in the transparent negligee she had worn last night when she had gone to Carlson's bed she stood up, the glass still in her hand, and walked unsteadily to the full length mirror on the back of the door to the adjoining bathroom. She looked at her own image and saluted herself mockingly with the glass. The old body hadn't started to go yet. At twenty-four, it was still as good as it had been at eighteen.

Margo Neal had packed a lot of living into those twenty-four years. She stared at herself, at the ripe, pointed breasts, the curving hips, the slender but stunning legs, and nodded thoughtfully as memories came unbidden and agonizingly.

She had been a junior in high school when her parents had told her the terrible news of their planned divorce. Up until then, her life had been extremely stable. Her father was an executive with an oil company; although he was away from home a great deal, his affection and attention during the brief periods when he was not traveling had made up to Margo for his absences.

But apparently he had not been able to make up to Margo's mother what she had been missing. Gina Neal was of Northern Italian extraction, and she was full of the smouldering passions inherited from generations of fiery and aristocratic ancestors. She craved more than the life of the patient waiter for an absentee husband and, still lovely at thirty-five, she had sought what she craved.

At the time, none of this had sunk in to Margo. Only much later, after her mother had vanished into some European limbo with one of her lovers, did Margo gradually begin to realize that her mother must have cheated consistently and frequently on her father from the early years of their marriage.

The divorce knocked the earth from under the child's feet. Suddenly she was floating adrift in a strange new world, a world where there was no stability and no standards. She reacted bitterly and violently. By the time her junior year was over she had been sent, by her father who was still enmeshed in the demands of his career, to an exclusive, all-girl school.

The high school principal had made the need for such action explicit to Margo's father A man who had stayed happily married himself, and who was genuinely concerned for children, the principal was, perhaps, a little more cutting with the elder Neal than courtesy would have normally allowed.

"You and your wife," he had told Clark Neal, "have left Margo nothing to cling to. Nothing at all. It's like turning the child adrift in the middle of the ocean with no paddle and no knowledge of navigation. The shore she seeks is love and security. But she doesn't know how to find it — and in the process she's about to blow our school apart."

"What do you mean?" Clark Neal had asked, sickly.

"Failing to get the love she needs at home, having lost all faith in that love," the principal said flatly, "Margo has turned to boys for it. Margo is promiscuous, Mr. Neal. She makes no secret of having had relations with half the senior boys of this school." He sighed. "Even at recess . . . behind the shrubbery on the school-ground."

Clark Neal's face was very white. "I — I didn't know. I have to be away so much. But I hired a housekeeper, someone to supervise her. . ."

"A housekeeper is not a mother," the principal said wearily. "Nor a father. Mr. Neal, Margo is a girl of great intelligence. Until — until this unpleasantness between yourself and your wife, we never had a moment's trouble with her. But I'm afraid now that the change in her has gone too far to be reversed easily. She will have to be put away from temptation and in a place where she will be more closely supervised. Now, I can recommend a girl's school at which she can finish her senior year and get her first two years of college. It's especially set up to take care of girls like Margo. The teachers are mature women who make it a point to establish very close relationship with the girls. The name of it is Ridgecroft . . ."

"Give me the details," Clark Neal had said numbly. "I'm going to be spending most of the next six months in South America. I've got to know that Margo is being looked after."

Ridgecroft. . . Margo Neal's lips twisted wryly as she remembered it. *That principal,* she thought. *He'd die if he really knew what he'd sent me into.*

"Wow," her roommate said, watching the newly arrived Margo undress. "Wow, you're really developed all the way. Look at those headlights."

The roommate's name was Shirley Kotten. She was a lean and rangy blonde of Margo's own age — sixteen. Her own breasts were small, almost nonexistent. Her eyes were a watery blue, her lips a weak and petulant puffiness. There was genuine envy in her eyes as she watched the nude Margo move cool and unashamed about the room. Envy ... and perhaps something else.

"You'll really be one of Miss Talbot's pets," Shirley added.

"I don't want to be anybody's pet here," Margo had snapped. "I think this is a stinking place. It's like a prison. No boys. What kind of place is a place without boys?"

Shirley gave a whinnying laugh.

"Miss Talbot will try to make it up to you."

Margo straightened, looked at Shirley. "Who's Miss Talbot?"

"She's the housemother for this dorm. She — she takes a real interest in all us girls."

Something in Shirley's voice struck Margo as secret and faintly coarse. She felt a pleasureable tingle of excitement, as if some unknown adventure were awaiting her.

"In fact," went on Shirley, "you could call this dorm Miss Talbot's harem."

"What?" Margo stared. Then, because she was neither naive nor ill-informed, she thought she began to see. "You mean ... ?"

Shirley laughed softly. "With boobs like that, you'll soon see what I mean. Just as soon as Miss Talbot gets a look at you."

Shirley had been right. It hadn't taken Miss Talbot long. Eve Talbot, twenty-eight, teacher of high school math, knew what she wanted. And when she saw Margo, Margo became what she wanted.

Margo was pacing the room on her very first night, feeling a great deal like a caged tiger. She did not know how she was going to be able to stand being shut in here away from men.

There was something inside her that seemed continually howling in anguish. Only when she was held tightly in the arms of someone else, only when there was an act of love being performed on her body did that howling subside. The howling was going on now, she did not know how long she could stand it without going crazy.

"Come on," Shirley said, from the bed where she was reading. "Time to hit the sack. Lights out in five minutes."

"Oh, all right," Margo grunted. She stripped off her clothes, slipped into a translucent nightgown old beyond her years. She crawled into her own bed and cut out the light.

"Good night," said Shirley.

"Good night," grunted Margo, and she stared into the darkness, not at all sleepy.

Her body was racked with tension, her muscles were taut with it. She closed her eyes, longing for someone to hold her. But there was no one. She had been put in this prison and now there was no one at all. She hugged herself, trying to imagine that her own arms were those of a boy, but it didn't work.

So she tried something else. She moved her hands over her breasts, slowly and caressingly, pretending that they were a boy's hands, too. She got no feeling of security, but a harsh pilot light of desire began to burn in her, and she felt her nipples harden against her own palms and she squeezed more tightly.

Her breathing began to be irregular. With her eyes tightly closed, she ran her hands down her flanks and over her stomach, tenderly. The anguished howling went on inside of her, flaring to a new crescendo as the desire her own hands engendered added its unfulfilled voice. Margo bit her lower lip tightly, as if in pain, and her buttocks moved back and forth across the sheet. One hand came back to her breasts, squeezing and pulling, more savagely now. The other hand dropped lower. Margo felt her legs moving of their own volition, and she began to rub her palm in a circular motion.

The sterile and mechanical desire rose higher. She squeezed her breasts with greater urgency, and the fingers of the other hand thrust and probed. Her body rose and fell on the bed, the springs made an embarrassing squeaking. From the other bed, Shirley giggled slightly, but said nothing.

At that moment, there was a knock on the door. A voice called softly: "Girls?"

"Ha," whispered Shirley. "She's here already."

Margo took her hands from her own body. Her brain fogged and swirling with desire, she lay rigid.

The door opened. "Girls, are you asleep?" Margo recognized the voice of Miss Talbot, whom she had just met that afternoon. She had a quick, mental picture of the woman: face strong-boned and handsome, hair close-cropped into a sandy shag, breasts small but distinct under the plain tweed jacket, waist and hips trim and slender, legs long. She had liked Miss Talbot at once, as much as she was able to like anybody any more who couldn't supply the love she need, the arms to hold her...

"No, Miss Talbot," Shirley said. "We're still awake."

Margo heard the pad of slippered feet, the rustle of robe. Then her bed sagged under a new weight as Miss

Talbot sat on the edge of it. "Margo?"

"Yes, Miss Talbot?" Margo closed her eyes tightly, wishing the woman would go away so she could finish what she had begun. But wondering, too, what the woman wanted with her, if she had correctly assessed Shirley's earlier cryptic remark.

"I always make it a practice to check in on new girls," Miss Talbot said gently. "A girl away from home on her first night is apt to be lonely and homesick. Are you lonely, Margo?"

"Yes, Miss Talbot," said Margo softly.

"Are you homesick?"

Margo thought for a moment.

"No," she said at last, bitterly.

"We don't want you to be lonely, Margo," Miss Talbot said. Suddenly, in a motherly fashion, her hand was stroking Margo's forehead, smoothing Margo's hair. Her hand was soft, but it seemed very strong.

"Thank you," Margo whispered. She was aware that Miss Talbot was bending over her, looking at her tenderly. Suddenly she sensed that Miss Talbot really cared, and all at once some of the tension went out of her.

Miss Talbot patted her shoulder. "It's a very lonely thing to be away from home for the first time, darling. But we'll try to make it up to you here."

"Yes," Margo said.

Miss Talbot's hand was stroking her neck now, caressing her throat. Instinctively, Margo moved the sheet so that Miss Talbot's hand would be free to slip lower.

The older woman understood the signal immediately, but she was unhurried. She stroked Margo's throat a moment longer. "There's really no need for you to be lonely.

None at all."

And as she murmured that, her hand slipped to Margo's breast.

Its touch started a flame in Margo that was like the holocaust of a fire roaring up a chimney. Her body went rigid, arched and dropped slightly. She heard a tiny sound of satisfaction in Eve Talbot's throat, and then the woman had her other hand on Margo's other breast, and she was caressing and loving those breasts exactly as a boy or a man would have.

"Margo," Miss Talbot whispered, and Margo felt Miss Talbot's hair brush her face, and then Miss Talbot's mouth was on hers, searching and demanding. Miss Talbot's hands more tightly against her breasts.

Without taking her mouth from the girl's, Eve Talbot freed her hands. The robe dropped away from her. Then she was under the sheet with Margo, and Margo felt the warmth of that lean body against her own, felt the weight of Miss Talbot's leg across her. Her own hands went out instinctively and found the older woman's apricot-sized breasts and rubbed them, and they hardened to her touch. Miss Talbot's breath was like explosion after explosion in Margo's mouth, and her tongue was relentless. Her hands traveled over Margo's body, stroking the white softness of Margo's belly, moving lower, and Margo tensed and moaned as Miss Talbot's fingers touched her expertly.

Then the Talbot woman had taken her mouth away from Margo's and her lips were traveling down Margo's throat. Eve Talbot's tongue traced out to Margo's nipples, leaving a warm wet trail. It circled each nipple then made its way to the cleft between Margo's breasts and wound down the length of her torso, slowly and caressingly. It was something that nobody had ever done to Margo before, and she liked it, and she felt her legs moving as Eve Talbot's sand-colored hair tickled her like the touch of feathers.

Then there was nothing else in the world but the older woman's caress and the astonishing things it was capable of, and Margo moaned and tossed in ecstasy, her hand behind Eve's head, pushing it hard against her.

Suddenly a new weight made the bed creak. All at once a new mouth was probing at Margo's own, new hands seized her breasts. She put out exploring fingers, found the nearly flat chest of Shirley. Then she was completely smothered in flesh, inundated by the attentions of the woman and the girl, both coming at once ...

And it was fine and it was good and it was exactly what she had been needing, arms holding her, two sets of arms; that they belonged to members of her own sex no longer mattered. She was wanted, desired, needed, and that was enough to quiet the howling, and when someone's body descended on her, when there was motion on either side of her head, she did not hesitate, but strained upward, her own mouth seeking and searching . . .

No, Margo Neal had not been lonely at the place called Ridgecroft.

She did not go on to her third year of college when she left Ridgecroft. By that time, she was well versed in just about every aspect of love. Ridgecroft was a hotbed of sexual activity, and though it was limited to members of the same sex, they worked infinite variations on it, many of which Margo knew, were, applicable to the art of love with a genuine and certifiable man.

But unlike many of the girls at Ridgecroft, Margo Neal, who'd had extensive experience with the real thing, never forgot that what they gave her at Ridgecroft was only a substitute. For her, it was simply something to use as a stopgap. When her hitch at Ridgecroft ended, instead of going home as she was supposed to do she struck out on her own. She had been deprived of the real thing too long. The anguished howling still went on within her. She had to search for something to make it stop permanently.

By that time, her father had given up on her. She was nineteen, and he let her lead her own life. He was too busy with his to do otherwise; in charge of foreign operations, his life was a whirl of jet-flights and hotel rooms. Margo had to seek her own salvation.

For the past five years, her life had been a blur of men. She had worked at no regular job, she had no regular or marketable skill except her skill in bed and her willingness to accept anything any man or woman wanted to do to her. She became a professional mistress. A man would support her (usually an aged man, because only they could afford it) for a year or two and then tire of her But inevitably, she was always passed along to a friend, so that she was never out of work, so to speak. And because most of the men were old, their demands on her minimal — usually only the last perverted desperate ones of old men trying to salvage from novelty their lost masculinity — she had plenty of time for younger men.

But none of them, young or old, had ever stopped the anguished howling in her.

Until last night.

For a while, in the arms of Carlson, it had quit completely. For the first time in years, it had died out absolutely for a while. Carlson was gone now, back to his island and his three native women, and, of course, the howling had come back, too — but, she wondered, would it be possible to stop it completely if only Carlson —?

Still looking at herself in the mirror she laughed harshly and mockingly and tossed off the rest of the drink.

Sure, she thought absurdly. *Sure, you can run barefoot and live on an island. Maybe that'll do it.*

"Admiring yourself, my dear?"

The door had opened behind her without warning, and she whirled to confront the squat, toadlike figure of George Marlowe. She forced a smile to her face.

"Hello, George."

He walked across the room toward her, his little red eyes devouring the lushness of her figure. "It was a pity," he grunted. "I got too drunk last night to do anything for you."

"Yes," she said. "You did."

"You sleep all right anyway?"

"I — ah, I had a hard time getting to sleep."

Marlowe's puffy lips twisted lewdly. "Yeah. You just have to have it. All day and all night. Don't you?" That, she knew, was what he liked to think. It excited him to think that she was absolutely insatiable.

She took a deep breath, afraid of what was coming now. But it was her job. "Yes," she said. "I always have to have it." And she deliberately moved her body against his, letting the tips of her breasts brush his shirt front, letting her body reach out to him.

She heard the hoarse, rasping snort of his breath in his nostrils. His eyes glittered. "Let me get it," he said, and he moved past her quickly to a locker. He opened the locker.

While he was behind her back and could not see her expression, Margo stood tautly, rigidly, with her eyes shut and a grimace of revulsion on her face. She was still standing like that, waiting for the inevitable, as he came toward her slowly, panting a little, the whip held tightly in his hands.

5

ALTHOUGH THE *lamua* WAS NOT TO START until sundown, the white men came ashore on Bora-Ka early in the afternoon. Farley had changed to a yachting cap, a blue tee-shirt, and khaki pants. The squat figure of George Marlowe was ludicrous in an aloha shirt that was an explosion of colors, and baggy Bermuda shorts. Carlson was not expecting them, and they interrupted his nap in the shade of a coconut palm.

When Valu shook him, he sat up groggily. "Oh," he

said, knuckling at his eyes. "Hello."

Farley held out a package. "We brought you a present."

"A present?" Carlson took it gingerly.

"Bottle of Scotch," said Farley.

Quickly, as if it were hot, Carlson handed it back. "No, thanks."

Farley's dark brows arched. "What's the matter? You seemed to enjoy it last night."

Carlson got to his feet a little stiffly. "Of course I enjoyed it. I like the stuff. But I don't want it on the island."

"Oh." Farley looked at him curiously for a moment. "Why not?"

"Let's just say these people have low thresholds," Carlson said coldly. "You remember what whiskey did to the Indians in the States? Well, it affects these people the same way and I don't want it around."

Farley shrugged affably. "Suit yourself. We just thought you'd like it — and, frankly, we were going to use it as a bribe."

Carlson's eyes narrowed. "A bribe?"

Farley chuckled. "Just to bribe you to give us a guided tour of the island. We'd like to see what a real South Seas island looks like."

Carlson relaxed a trifle. His eyes shuttled to Marlowe. Marlowe had his attention riveted on Valu's breasts. Carlson did not like the expression on Marlowe's fat face. Suddenly anxious to get Marlowe out of the village, he said, "All right. But there's not much to see."

"Whatever there is, we'd like to see it."

Carlson nodded. "All right. Come along. There are

no vehicles, it will be a walking tour."

"I guess there's no help for that," said Farley. "George? George? Come along. Mr. Carlson's going to show us over the island." He grinned at Carlson. "George Marlowe is an appreciator of beauty."

"The beauty he happens to be appreciating right now," said Carlson thinly, "happens to be my wife."

"Yes, of course," said Farley hastily. "George means no harm. George?"

"The island," said Carlson, as they struck inland away from the beach, "is about ten miles long and five miles wide. It's the biggest island of the Bora-Ka group, and the only really habitable one."

"Why is that?" asked Marlowe, who seemed to have forgotten women now, and whose eyes searched the terrain about them.

Carlson gestured to the path they followed. It led uphill, between walls of tropical growth.

"This is the only island with any rise in the center," he said. "It's the only one high enough to offer protection against typhoons."

"Typhoons? Do you get many of those?"

"Not many," said Carlson. "But when they do come, they inundate the atoll. The other islands are sometimes completely covered by water. But the center of Bora-Ka is high enough to offer refuge."

"When was the last typhoon?"

"There hasn't been one since I've been here. We're out of the usual route those things seem to follow. But I understand that right after the war, they had a dilly."

"One in what? Fifteen, sixteen, seventeen years?

That doesn't seem like much."

"I'm talking about typhoons," Carlson told him. "Hurricanes. We get our share of rough enough storms as it is. They don't reach typhoon velocity, but they can make life pretty sticky for a while."

They toiled upward, the ground rising more steeply now. A cliff-like wall or rock thirty feet high rose before them, crowning the island.

"It looks like even a little storm would blow down those huts," said Farley. Marlowe was panting too hard to talk.

"Usually, a storm will. But the islanders figure what the hell? It only takes a day to build them back, and they don't have anything else to do anyway."

"I see," said Farley. "What's that hole in the cliff yonder?" He pointed to a gaping darkness visible behind the tropical greenery.

"That's the cave," said Carlson. "The only cave on the island. It's kept stocked with food and water. When a really bad blow comes along, the islanders take refuge in there and ride it out. It's above the level of the highest tides."

"Um-hmh." Farley pointed to the level plateau at the top of the cliff. "Does that run the whole length of the island?"

"It's an old volcanic formation, sort of what they call a *mesa* in the Southwest, back in the States. It's about three miles long."

"Is there a path up?"

"Yeah." Carlson glanced at Marlowe. "Pretty steep climb, though." Marlowe was bright red of face and puffing heavily.

"I can make it," Marlowe grunted. He started up the path ahead of them.

Farley let him gain some distance. "Nothing stops George," he said with admiration in his voice. "Nothing. When he starts out to go somewhere, he goes. When he wants something, he gets it. Did you know that he's one of the wealthiest men in the United States?"

"So what?" Carlson said flatly. "He's a long way from home right now. Come on." They followed Marlowe up the path.

When they reached the table-top which was clear of growth, level as a football field, though grassed thickly, Marlowe had already gained it and was puffing hard, trying to get back his wind. But his head was turning this way and that, and his eyes were narrowed and he seemed lost in thought.

As Farley and Carlson came up, Marlowe nodded. "Uh-huh," he muttered to himself. "There's plenty of room for the landing strip."

Carlson stared at him. "The what?"

"The landing strip," Marlowe said a trifle impatiently.

Carlson whirled on Farley, feeling the smart of anger, the knowledge that something they had not mentioned before was in their minds. "What the hell's he taking about?"

Farley gave him a white-toothed grin and raised a placatory hand. "Now, don't get all excited, Carlson," He gestured to an outcropping of rocks. "Let's sit down over there and have a little pow-wow. George and I have a little scheme. But we didn't want to mention it until George was sure this was the place for it. I think he's sure now. Aren't you, George?"

"Yeah," Marlowe grunted.

"I want to know what this is all about!" Carlson clenched his fists and looked from Farley to Marlowe.

"Well, relax, sit down, and we'll tell you," said Farley. He led the way to the rocks, took a flask from his hip pocket. and sat down. He offered the flask to Carlson, who shook his head.

Farley shrugged and drank and passed the flask to Marlowe, who sank down on the rocks with a sigh of relief and drank greedily.

Farley waited a beat or two before speaking. At last, he said: "We're going to make you a rich man, Carlson."

Rod Carlson stared, uncomprehendingly.

"The availability of this as a landing strip fitted the last piece of the jigsaw puzzled into place. Carlson, we've spent the past three months touring every out of the way island in the Pacific, looking for something exactly like this. Bora-Ka is the first place we've found that meets our specifications exactly. Right, George?"

"Right," grunted Marlowe. He took another swig from the flask.

"Specifications for what?" Carlson's voice was a whisper.

"For the kind of resort we intend to build."

For a moment Farley's words hung unanswered in the air. Then Carlson said slowly, a dawn of comprehension tinging his voice, "A resort? On Bora-Ka?"

"That's right. Look, Carlson. You've been to Tahiti. You know what a crummy place it is. Every tourist that hits there is disappointed. The French have let it turn into a bunch of honky-tonks and off-breed girls with bad teeth. And still — Tahiti, or a South Sea island like it — remains everybody's dream of escape. Just — just as it was yours."

"Go on," said Carlson thinly.

Farley shrugged. "It's simple. It's simple as hell, and there's a pile of money in it for everybody, including you. We'll build accommodations on the various islands. Huts, sort of like the ones your natives live in, but with more privacy and running water and flush toilets. We'll build a regular hotel, too, for the people who don't want to live in the huts. We'll have a cocktail lounge and a gambling casino. And a night club, and we'll book the best acts to play it — we're prepared to pay more than the clubs in Vegas, even. We'll turn Bora-Ka into the kind of place Tahiti should be, but isn't. There'll be hydrofoil ferries across the lagoon to the various islands. We'll make beachboys out of your men and we'll put all your women to work, too. The pretty ones, I'm sure, can make themselves a fortune. Of course, with only two hundred natives total on the island, there won't be enough pretty girls. But we can import a couple of hundred more from Hawaii, and we'll bring in some more native beefcake, too. Because if there's one thing the tourists like, it's a nice strong native boy for Mama and a nice soft native girl for Papa, and that's what they're looking for when they come to a place like this. Romance under the palms, with the tropical seas lapping gently on the shore, and the native drums throbbing from the casino in the background. You know the bit. Hell, man, Bora-Ka's made to order for it. And George and I have already talked it over — we'll make you our manager if you'll help us set the deal up with the natives."

For a moment, Rod Carlson was absolutely speechless, his brain paralyzed by the enormity of what Farley was proposing.

Farley saw the stricken look on his face.

"Hell, don't worry. We'll weed out the riff-raff. This place will be for people for whom Miami Beach is too cheap and ordinary. Look, this is all the rage now. There's a movie star who's started a place like that in Kenya; people want to travel, they want to go places and they get tired of the same places over and over. Jet airliners have brought places like this and Kenya within the reach of everybody. Sooner or later, somebody's going to develop Bora-Ka, and we want to be the ones to do it."

He stood up and patted Carlson on the shoulder in the manner of one conspirator greeting another. "Listen, man, you must have got tired of this native stuff. In another two years, if you help us, there'll be more nice white vacationing stuff just yearning for it running around this island than you can shake a stick — or anything else — at. You'll pretty nearly be your own boss and you'll be cut in for fifteen per cent of the take. How does that sound?"

Carlson flung his arm off coldly. "It sounds rotten," he said thinly.

Farley's grin faded. Marlowe looked up keenly.

"Listen," Carlson grated. "These people have a good life here as it is. They don't need your night club and your casino and your hydrofoil ferries and your tired American nymphos and satyrs. All they need is taro and the fish out of the lagoon and the sunshine and the sea. They're not corrupted, do you understand, Farley?

They've never been corrupted, nothing's ever touched them to corrupt them — and I'll not let them be corrupted now. You and Marlowe and your resort can go to some other island, or to hell. You're not setting up shop on Bora-Ka."

Marlowe let out a snort through his nostrils. He stood up, red eyes glittering.

"Big talk, Mister. Do you own Bora-Ka?"

"No. Neither do you. It's maintained to the United States by the U.N."

Marlowe's puffy lips curled in an unpleasant smile. "You think I can't get development rights to it? You think the government wouldn't like to see these underdeveloped, underprivileged people brought out of the dark ages by private enterprise? Listen, Mister; I've cut timber in National Forests, I've secured oil rights in National Parks. I've swung some real deals in my time. The day I can't get hold of a lousy little island lost in this lousy ocean, I'll go out of business and fire all my boys in Washington."

"The hell you will!" Carlson flared. "You'll get the hell off this island before I throw you off!"

"I'd like to see you try it?" Farley snapped, taking a step forward. "You ever see a karate expert in action, Carlson? It's become quite popular since you left the States."

Marlowe put a thick-fingered hand on Farley's arm. "Hold it, Lloyd. This jerk is nothing. Hell, he's not even the headman on this island. That old buzzard with the tattoos named Halu is. He's the one we'll deal with."

Carlson swung toward Marlowe. "I'll tell Halu to throw you in the lagoon —"

Marlowe shook his head slowy. "I don't think Halu will do that. I brought him another boatload of presents when we came ashore. He promised me the courtesy of the island as long as I wanted to stay. That might be a long time, Carlson."

Carlson was seething with anger and sick at heart as he ran through the underbrush and came out in the level, open space between the palms. Ahead of him, he saw the huts of the village. They looked as they always had, as he remembered them from the first time he had seen them. But now, as he jogged toward the headman's quarters, he was struck by how flimsy and impermanent they seemed.

He found Halu sitting cross-legged in front of his hut, watching his wives clean fish for the *lamua*. Halu looked up in surprise as Carlson approached.

"My son," he greeted Carlson. "You are red of face and short of breath. Why do you run? Where are our two white friends?"

"They're coming," Carlson grated. "I left them behind. My father, I must talk to you." He sat cross-legged in front of Halu.

"What disturbs you, my son?" Halu looked at him with kindly eyes.

"The white men disturb me." Carlson talked rapidly, trying to explain what Farley and Marlowe had told him. Halu listened closely, but without the faintest comprehension on his face. It dawned on Carlson as he talked that there were no terms at his command with which he could explain Marlowe's scheme. Halu had seen an occasional airplane, but never a jet airliner. He had no idea what a night club was, nor a tourist resort. Gambling, he vaguely comprehended; there was a very mild form of it, not unlike bingo, indigenous to the island.

"But I don't see why you're so upset," he told Carlson. "If visitors come, we welcome them. If they need to borrow women, we will lend them ours."

"But you don't understand . . ." Carlson gestured. "There will be too many of them. The island will no longer belong to the people of Bora-Ka. It will belong to others, and your people — our people — will be only servants for them."

He had to use the English word *servants*. There was no such word in the Bora dialect, and the futility of it suddenly depressed him. Halu still did not understand.

"Look," Carlson said desperately. "The white men will come and talk to you. They will ask you for favors. Please do not grant them unless I say it is all right."

Halu frowned. "But one always grants favors to guests. It is the custom. And as for your saying it is all right — with all due respect, my son, I remain the headman of the island." He smiled reassuringly and patted Carlson's knee. "Do not worry, my son. It is too hot to be so red in the face. Go now and put your head on the breast of one of my daughters and take a nap. Then swim in the cool ocean. Then go to your house and prepare for the *lamua*. It will be a fine and ornate one. I have mustered all our resources, for the white friends have brought us many wonderful presents."

Carlson stood up, shaking his head helplessly. "You just won't understand, will you?" he said in English. "You're just too good. to unspoiled to comprehend." He sucked in a deep breath. "All right. If they have to be fought, I'll just have to do it myself. And I will fight them." He looked at the ocean, placid in the sunlight. Far out on its surface, a little rain squall galloped along the horizon like a frisky colt. The sun shining through it made it glitter with yellow, blue, and r_?, like a transient rainbow.

"I'll fight them," Carlson said again. "I'll fight them with everything I've got, and I'll kill them or they'll have to kill me before I'll let 'em ruin Bora-Ka." Then he turned and trudged slowly toward his hut, still churning inside with those emotions so foreign to this island — anger and fear.

6

THE SKY WAS A VAST IMMENSITY ARCHING
over the ocean, a huge, dark bowl, spangled
with glittering points of silver. The sea
caught the reflection of the starlight and the
moonlight and gave it back in broken and shining ripples.
As the small boat carried them across the reef, Joyce
Marlowe said: "What kind of brawl is this we're supposed to be going to?"

"Some kind of native orgy," her sister Anne said.
"You know. Like in the movies. Hula dances and all that

jazz."

"They call it a *lamua*," Margo Neal said quietly from the other end of the boat.

"I don't care what they call it," Anne giggled. "I just hope there're lots and lots of those gorgeous beach boys there."

"Leave some for me," Joyce tittered.

Margo Neal turned away from them and looked out at the black bulk of the island approaching quickly from the distance. Already there was faintly audible the sound of drums, and as the boat moved inshore, she could see the winking light of a huge bonfire. Somewhere a girl was singing a plaintive native chant in a high falsetto.

A shiver went down Margo Neal's spine. It was beautiful and primitive. But the shiver was not caused by that. It was caused by the knowledge that Rod Carlson was somewhere there in the darkness and that tonight she might see him again.

The boat beached on the soft, yielding sand. "All right, ladies," the steersman said. He got out and lent them a helping hand.

"We should have worn our sarongs," Joyce said as they stepped onto the beach. The drumming was louder now, and several voices had taken up the chant.

"I don't have a sarong," Anne laughed. "But I didn't wear any panties."

"Neither did I," said Joyce.

Margo heard the steersman make a sound in his throat. She felt no pity for him. She knew that he had enjoyed both the Marlowe sisters during the cruise. Every sailor aboard had, at one time or another. The two girls were genuine nymphomaniacs, she thought.

And I? What can I? she wondered as she went up the white sand. She was barefoot carrying her shoes in her hands. *Who am I to talk?*

A figure appeared out of the darkness; it was Rod Carlson. "Hello," he said. He took Margo's hand. "This way to the festivities."

Margo gave his hand a squeeze, her heart pounding at his nearness, the anguished howling in her rising, then subsiding a bit. "It looks dreadfully primitive and exciting," she said. "Like something out of a movie."

"It may get more primitive before the night is over," said Carlson fiercely.

She looked at him in the darkness as they entered the coconut grove, but she could not make out his expression. "What do you mean?"

"I mean," he grated, "something new has been added. By your friends. I told them to keep whiskey off this island. But it seems they went ahead and brought a case of gin with them. And now all the islanders are swigging gin — something they've never had before. God knows what it will do to them."

Margo sucked in her breath in sympathy. "I'm sorry."

"For hundreds of years," Carlson said with savagery, "For hundreds of years these people have lived here uncorrupted and harming no one. They're sexually free, but they have no knowledge of abnormality. They're open-handed and generous and don't know what money is. They're happy, in short. But your boys from the yacht seem determined to fix all that. Your great and good friends Marlowe and Farley seem determined to educate them in a hurry."

"I'm sorry," she said again.

"It's all right," he said bitterly. "I don't suppose you had anything to do with it. But you'd better stay close to me tonight. I don't have any idea what these people are going to do when that gin strikes home."

Ahead of them, Margo saw the bonfire. It was huge; spread out, to light up the interior of the whole grove. Its yellow reflection played and danced on the shiny palm leaves overhead, and around it, in circular ranks, sat the islanders of Bora, the firelight playing across the soft, bare, brown breasts of the women, and the hard, muscle-banded chests of the men.

Carlson led Margo to a spot in front of the fire. "Margo," he said in English, "these are my wives, Kama, Tesai, and Valu." In the dialect, he said: "My wives there is one of the white women from the yacht. She is the one whom I borrowed last night. Make her welcome."

Smiling nervously Margo allowed herself to be drawn down among the bare-breasted women. Carlson seated himself nearby. Across the fire, in what was evidently the place of honor, Margo saw the headman, Halu, whom she had glimpsed that morning on the yacht. On either side of him sat Marlowe and Farley. Marlowe did not appear to miss Margo. He had one arm around a native girl who could not have been over fifteen and was nuzzling her neck and squeezing one small and pliant naked breast. Farley had an older girl, perhaps all of twenty, and, though not as blatant as Marlowe, his hand still played up and down her torso, while she smiled complaisantly, proud to have been designated an instrument of courtesy to the visitors.

Then Halu stood up, a hollowed-out coconut in his hands, and began to talk. His voice rose and fell in liquid, flowery syllables. Margo leaned close to Carlson. "What's he saying?"

"He's making a speech of welcome," Carlson whispered tersely. "Very flowery."

A native girl appeared before Margo as Halu orated on. She extended a hollowed-out coconut similar to the one Halu held.

"What's this?" asked Margo.

"It's the only kind of drinking glass there is on the island." Carlson's voice took on an edge. "Don't expect anything exotic. It's full of warm gin."

Margo took it, sipped it and grimaced. What he had said was true. But the fiery touch of it was soothing as it struck home in her stomach, and she took another swallow of it.

The girl brought coconuts for Valu, Tesai, and Kama.

Carlson shook his head. "No," he said harshly.

Tesai pouted. "Please, my husband. Let us try the white man's drink."

"Please," chimed in Valu.

Carlson looked at them for a moment, then made a helpless gesture. His face, in the firelight, was quite grim. "All right," he said in the dialect. "Drink it. But don't blame me if you become sick." He looked at Margo. "I hope they all get so sick off it they never want to touch it again."

"You're not drinking," she said.

"There's no telling what this will turn into," he said. "Somebody's got to stay sober."

She held out her coconut. "Have a sip of mine."

"No."

"One won't hurt you." She was aroused by his nearness. She wanted him desperately, but she could see that he was in no mood for romance. He was too angry, too apprehensive, too hurt. The gin would be good for him. It would relax him.

He took the coconut. "I'll have one. Because Halu's going to take a ceremonial drink in a moment, and all the men are supposed to drink with him. I don't want him to think I'm discourteous. That's the gravest sin you can commit on this island — discourtesy."

At that moment, Halu's oration broke off. Margo guessed that nobody but she had as yet tasted the gin. The three native girls by her were sitting quietly with their coconuts cradled between their folded legs. Probably Halu's drink would be the signal for the islanders to have their first taste of gin.

As Halu's words died, a shout went up from the men of Bora. There was something wild and primitive and masculine in it that frightened Margo slightly and twitched the short hairs on the back of her neck. Then Halu was grinning broadly and ostentatiously raising the coconut to his lips.

He drank deeply as he would have of the native wine. Then, spluttering and choking and grimacing, he lowered the coconut quickly, trying to conceal his reaction, for to show distaste would have been discourteous. His face was a study in surprise and shock for an instant, but the fiery gin bit into him quickly, and all at once a slow, beatific smile spread over his face and he nodded approvingly and drank again, not quite so deeply this time.

At that signal, the second drink, all the islanders followed suit. Beside her, Margo heard muffled exclamations of surprise from Carlson's wives. "Ai," Valu said in dialect. "It is like the sting of the toadfish."

Tesai let out a shuddering breath. "Fire," she murmured. "Fire in my belly." She shivered, breasts bobbing. "But how it warms within. I can feel a strange tingling."

"It is a pleasant feeling. The taste is not good, but the feeling is most pleasant," Kama added.

Carlson had taken only a sip. He handed the coconut back to Margo. "Here," he said. "You can have it." He turned his back on her and stared moodily into the fire.

Margo's lips thinned. *All right*, she thought bitterly. *So it was just a one-night stand. What did you expect, Margo Neal?* Suddenly, impulsively, she raised the coconut and drank long and deep.

Halu had sat down. He drank again, chortled, and then clapped his hands and said something loud. The drummers, who beat on hollowed-out palm logs with sticks, increased their tempo.

"Now what happens?" Margo asked, her voice a trifle thick. She could feel the burn of the gin radiating out to breasts and loins.

"Now, they will dance the *Remeru.*"

"What's the *Remeru?*"

"It's a love dance," said Carlson tersely. "Very romantic. The women dance the first movement. The men dance the second. Then they all dance the third together."

"What happens then?"

Carlson turned his head and looked at her steadily.

"What do you *think* happens?"

"Oh," said Margo softly. To cover her confusion, she took another drink from the coconut. She was aware of Valu, Tesai, and Kama doing likewise. "Will you dance?" she asked when she lowered the drink.

"I'm supposed to," said Carlson tersely.

Margo felt a touch of hope. "May I dance, too?"

Carlson looked at her quickly. His face was expressionless in the firelight. "That's up to you. Maybe you'd better watch for a while first."

Beside Margo, the three girls were getting to their feet. Margo heard the soft rustle of fabric as the *pareus* they wore around their waist dropped.

"I have never felt more like dancing than I do tonight," Tesai said in the island language.

"Strange, but it is the same with me," giggled Valu.

"It must be the white man's drink," said Kama. "It is a good drink. I like it very much."

"Come, my sisters, let us dance," said Tesai. "The white man's drink has filled me with fire."

Margo watched them as they moved out into the firelight. From the ranks around the blaze, other women were also arising, all nude. A trifle unsteadily, they all moved out into the circle of open space between fire and onlookers.

Halu drank deeply from his coconut and gave a piercing shout. The throb of the drums grew louder. Margo moved closer to Carlson, watching wide-eyed. She drank again.

She saw a phantasmagoria unfolding before her eyes. Highlighted by the fireglow, all the young native women were beginning to dance. They danced not with their

feet but with their bodies. They kept their feet station-
ary. At first only their hands moved, in graceful gestures
not unlike those of the hula. But, as if spreading from
the hands to the rest of their bodies, a slow, sensuous
rhythm set their torsoes to swaying. Their breasts shone
in the firelight, rippling gently.

Then their hips began to move from side to side.
Still this was all in slow motion. If this was what the
dance was like, it would be dull stuff, Margo thought.

Then the drums abruptly changed tempo, going into
a staccato beat totally unlike their previous rhythm. And
the circle around the fire exploded into action.

Margo saw the women spread their legs; their whole
bodies began to shake furiously. Their breasts bobbed
and swayed and jounced. Their hips ground back and
forth in quick, simulated passion; the slap of their buttocks was clearly audible. Their heads were thrown back,
their eyes closed, long black hair swirled and fanned.

As if at a common signal, the girls grabbed their
breasts in their hands and squeezed. Their hips did incredible things, arching and twisting. Their feet moved
swiftly all the while.

The drumming grew swifter, still with that off beat.
It was obvious what the island women were doing. With
their own hands and bodies they were working themselves up to a receptive pitch of passion.

Their hands traveled, unashamed, all over their own
bodies, which now were swirling, twisting, stamping blurs
in the high leaping firelight. None touched another, but
each aroused only herself. Margo felt a tension grow in
her own breasts, and, involuntarily, she put her hands
to them and squeezed. She closed her eyes, enjoying the

ripple of ecstasy that went through her. It seemed that the beat of the drums exactly matched the thrum of blood in her temples.

Then suddenly all the women sank, nearly exhausted, to the ground, heads bowed.

And as if at a common signal, the men arose then. Only Carlson and Halu remained where they sat, as did, of course, Marlowe and Farley. All the other island men of dancing age strutted into the center, quite as nude as the women had been, and danced among the women.

Margo pressed her legs together tightly as she watched that spectacle. The men were magnificent male animals, each already aroused by the dance of the women. They cavorted quite as explicitly and unashamed as the women had, dancing over and around the women's sprawled bodies.

Margo felt as if she were on fire. She looked at Carlson, who sat rigidly with his back toward her. She snarled an oath deep in her throat, an oath of frustration. Desire and that old anguish were howling within her. She drained the coconut. Her hands went to the buttons of the blouse she'd worn.

The hell with Carlson! She had to quiet that howling within her.

Then the women were rising to greet the men. Margo saw that Joyce and Anne Marlowe had already anticipated her. Long golden hair shining, eyes glittering, they stepped nude out of the crowd, to join with the native women who were getting to their feet. The drum beats increased yet again in tempo. The two Marlowe girls began to dance with the islanders. Their white breasts joggled, rose tips shining. Their white hips and buttocks swayed and ground. The islanders marveled at the gyrating thighs, quite unlike anything they had ever seen before.

"Yowee!" Margo heard Anne Marlowe yell. "I'm ready! Who's for it?"

Her father did not even look up from the native girl he was bearing over backward.

Margo's hands fumbled clumsily with the rest of her clothes. An eternity seemed to pass before they dropped from her; then she felt the caress of the cool night against bare skin. The world wheeling tipsily about her, she danced out into the circle.

She saw Carlson raise a startled head. He stared at her, and she gave him a spiteful smile, and then she shut her eyes and abandoned herself to the savage frenzy of the dance.

She played her own hands all over her own body screamed for the touch of a male—any male. She twisted and squirmed and shook, quite lost in a fog of passion, determined to show Carlson what he was missing.

Suddenly the drumbeat stopped. Margo opened her eyes.

She was staring into the face of a strongly-built island youth. The admiration and lust in his expression were plain to see. Margo moaned and threw herself against him.

Then she was picked up in strong arms. All around her, the same thing was happening to the other women. There were not enough men to go around, but for each woman picked up, two more trotted alongside as the man carried the woman into the darkness of the coconut grove.

Margo closed her eyes and let herself be carried.

Then she felt the harsh rasp of old coconut fronds against her back and buttocks. She did not care. Instinctively, she reached up for the man above her, drew him down to her.

He was huge and strong and magnificent, and his stallion-like efforts sent ripple after ripple of ecstasy through her body. Once she screamed with the sheer racking release of it. And finally, when he was through, she was, for the moment, exhausted.

The man immediately stood up. He seized one of the two women who had followed them into the grove and carried her deeper into the darkness. The last woman trotted alongside. Margo lay where he had left her, staring up at the sky.

Slowly, strength and a measure of sanity returned to her, though she knew she was still very, very drunk. She sighed and closed her eyes.

The island man had been good, very good.

But he had not been Carlson.

"Hey," Joyce Marlowe said when the man got off of her. "Is that all?"

The man said something in that liquid dialect of theirs. Joyce reached out to seize him, but he eluded her grasp and picked up her sister Anne, who had followed, and carried Anne into the darkness. A native girl went along too.

Joyce sat up, cursing silently. Why, she had just got started good. He had hardly damped the fire within her at all.

Joyce Marlowe was very drunk. And when Joyce Marlowe was very drunk, one man was just an *hors d'oeuvre*. She had been like that for as long as she could remember and so had Anne. *Probably*, she thought drunkenly, *something inherited from the old man*. He was quite the lecherous old goat himself — him and that big-boobed Margo.

Joyce got unsteadily to her feet. Through the coconut palms, she could see the glitter of the fire. Maybe, she thought, maybe there's a man there...a man I could get. And I'd better hurry before that joker gets through with Anne. Because she'll be back on the run, too. She'll want seconds too.

She lurched into the firelight. The area was clear of people now except Halu, Farley, Carlson, and her father. She grinned crookedly. *Look at the old goat...* He was rolling around on the ground with a bronze girl, his body heaving ludicrously and with futility. Joyce stared at him with hatred and spite in her eyes. Marlowe had corrupted his own daughters at an early age. He had encouraged them in the nourishing of the violent appetites that churned in them, getting a perverted pleasure out of watching his own children become libertines. *Well, we're what he wants*, Joyce thought fuzzily. Her eyes flickered to Farley. He, too, was locked in an embrace with one of the bronze women. The headman, Halu, had no woman. He just had a coconut shell, from which he drank long and deeply. A stupid grin on his face, he rocked back and forth on his buttocks, obviously stone drunk and nearly helpless.

Only Carlson sat apart, his face hard and grim and bitter, his eyes steely with sobriety.

Joyce staggered over to him and dropped to her knees beside him. She took one of her big, naked breasts in her hand and rubbed its point against his cheek, brought the hard tip of it around under his nose and drew it across his lips. "Sugar," she said, her other hand reaching out and searching boldly. "Sugar, come on with me. Little Joyce needs you bad. Real bad."

He stared up at her opaquely. With one big hand, he pushed her breast away; with the other, he stopped the searching of her fingers. "Get away from me," he said coldly.

Joyce drew back from him, lips curling away from teeth in a snarl. "Why, you big so-and-so." Suddenly she turned supplicant. "Please," she begged. She dropped before him and put her head in his lap. "Please, please, please. . ." Her voice died away in a mumble.

Carlson made a sound in his throat. He got his hands under her shoulders and lifted her. "Get away," he said again, roughly. When she remained dead weight, he threw her from him. She went sprawling on the ground.

With that unquenched flame still burning in her, she shook her head groggily. "Damn you," she breathed. But she knew that Carlson meant it, that he would not give her what she needed.

She got to her knees, brushed the bits of palm frond from her buttocks. The case of gin sat before the fire. She seized a half-empty bottle from it and pushed herself to her feet. "Awright," she mumbled. "Awright, you cold fish. . ." Aimlessly she lurched from the clearing.

She emerged onto the beach. Before her, the white sand and the ocean stretched away under a flood moonlight. She was aware that there were other people on the beach, too — women, those taken first, as she had been, now on their way to cleanse themselves in the ocean. She heard their tipsy giggling, their magpie chatter as they ran into the water and let it lave them.

Joyce uncorked the gin bottle and took a long drag of the clear, pungent liquid. It exploded in her like a thousand rockets going off, and she muttered: "Oh, hell," because the wanting now was even more intense. She staggered down the beach, still clutching the bottle, and splashed into the water.

It was very warm and its gentle motion was like a million warm wet tongues lapping at her body. A shudder of excitement went over her and she closed her eyes.

Then somebody said something next to her in the island language. There was a pull at the gin bottle she held, and she looked up to see one of the native girls tugging at the bottle. Vaguely she recognized the girl as one of the three who had sat with Carlson, one of his wives. This was the one with the largest breasts.

"Please," Tesai said thickly in the dialect. "Please, let me have some more of the good drink." Her brain was reeling; something very strange and magical was happening in her head. It was all due to the white liquid that was like fire, and she craved it deeply, with a craving she had never known before. "Please," she said again.

Joyce stared at her, eyes taking in the round, small-nosed face, the sensual lips, the heavy breasts like bronze carvings, their tips jutting from silver dollar-sized aureoles. Native or not, this girl was a knockout... A sudden and entirely wicked idea fastened itself in Joyce's brain. "Sure," she said, and she turned loose of the gin bottle.

What she planned was not something she ordinarily preferred. But at a time like this, she told herself blurrily, any old port in a storm...

She watched the native girl drink deeply of the stuff. "Hey," Joyce said, "you're gonna knock yourself out." But the girl paid no attention. Joyce had to drag the bottle away from her. The girl hiccuped and looked at her with glazed eyes. Joyce also drank.

While she was drinking, Tesai stared at the white body waist deep in water, glimmering in the moonlight. What large breasts, Tesai thought blurrily. How white and soft, white as the meat of coconut... She put out a curious hand and touched Joyce's left breast.

Joyce lowered the bottle and stared at Tesai. "Hey," she mumbled, "maybe you know more than I gave you credit for." Suddenly, with a wild gesture, she flung the empty gin bottle far up on the beach, and then, before Tesai could move, she seized the island girl and pulled her to her.

Vaguely, Tesai was startled. What strange gesture was this, between women? She felt her own breasts crush against those big, white, soft ones. It was not unpleasant. And Joyce's mouth was bearing down on hers before she could move her head.

For a moment Tesai thought, with the tiny part of her mind that was still functioning, that she should push the white woman away. But that would have been discourteous. Besides —

Lips and tongue probed and thrust at her mouth. Something very strange was happening. It was as if Tesai stood on the beach and watched herself in the water. No conscious volition made her own mouth open; no conscious volition made her push her body against the white woman's.

Then, still locked like that, they were somehow

through the shallows and up on the beach. Joyce bore
Tesai over backward. Tesai's legs were very unsteady,
they yielded promptly and she landed on her shoulders in
the sand.

Some of the other women saw what was happening.
All of them very drunk, they gathered about to watch.

Tesai kept her eyes closed. The white woman was
doing strange things to her. Things nobody had ever done
before, things she had never dreamed of. Now the white
woman's mouth was on her breasts, the white woman's
hand was at her legs. Rippling shudders of enjoyment
went through Tesai. Surely it was unheard of for one
woman to behave like this with another. But the whites
had so many weird customs — and now, even if she had
wanted to stop the white woman, she was powerless to.
She was so excited herself that her body would not obey
her mind in anything, and the whole world seemed to
be rocking and swaying crazily.

The white woman's mouth had left her breasts now,
and the white woman's hands were there instead. Tesai
opened her eyes at the trace of soft hair moving across
her stomach. She watched curiously as the blonde head
moved lower.

Above her, she heard the other women making exclamations of wonderment. "What a thing to see!" "What
a thing to do!" Then Tesai sucked in a long breath and
almost screamed. She closed her eyes, and, instinctively,
her hand pushed hard against Joyce's head, bearing it
tightly against her. The earth rocked and lurched at a
faster rhythm, now, and nobody, not even Carlson, had
ever made her feel quite this frantic in such an odd way.

And then there was explosion after explosion in Tesai

and something else was happening. The white woman **had** fallen back on the sand. Her body was arched, waiting. Tesai stared. The white woman wanted her to do the same thing...

And the white woman had made her feel so wonderful that it was only courtesy to reciprocate...

The other women, watching, were curiously excited by what they saw. Tentatively, some of them began to touch others. The others responded with alacrity or hesitance, depending upon the amount of gin within them. But it was something new and curious and seemed to be enjoyable, and the credo of Bora-Ka was that anything really enjoyable was not taboo. So that other couples sank to the sand, experimentally at first, then, in moments, lost in growing excitement.

The huge moon that bathed the beach in silver shone down on bronze bodies writhing together, and in their midst one white one, still desperate, still insatiable, urging them all on to greater efforts as if taking some deep inner joy in corruption.

7

"**A**I, MY SON," SAID HALU, THE HEADMAN. "My skull feels like a coconut that has lain in the hot sun too long. Surely, if it were opened, everything inside would be found to have fermented."

"It is the aftereffects of the white man's drink," Carlson said without sympathy. "Always, when too much is drunk of that drink, this occurs."

Halu rubbed his temples. They were sitting in his hut; the headman's eyes would not tolerate the sunlight.

"Does one die from it?"

"No," Carlson said with a icy smile tugging at his lips. "One is not given that relief. One does not die. One only wishes one would."

"Still," Halu mumbled, "it is a most joyous potion. Do the white men drink it all the time?"

"Some of them," said Carlson. "But to do so is not good. It robs one of strength and though it gives one wild dreams of manhood, it takes away the means of fulfilling them."

"Surely a magic drink," said Halu. "I hope the white men have more of it. Even though it hurts afterward, the feeling of happiness it brings is worth it."

"Look," Carlson said intensely. "When one drinks it, one loses all judgment. The people of Bora-Ka do not need the white man's drink to bring them happiness. They have happiness already."

"After a fashion," said Halu. "But it is plain that the white man has more happiness than we. He has all he wants of the magical drink. And he has women who are tall and big of breast. Did you not see the three white women dance last night and was it not an exciting thing to see?"

Carlson stared at him.

"My father," he said at last, "of all the things needed by the headman of the Bora people, the white man's drink and the white man's women are the least necessary. They should be declared taboo by the priests."

"Oh, no," said Halu quickly, and then he winced. In a moment he went on. "I shall let nothing that enjoyable be declared taboo." He groped around until he found a gin bottle. There was an inch of clear liquid left in it.

"Perhaps this will rid me of this miserable ache and bring back happiness." He uncorked the bottle and put it to his mouth and drained it. He gagged violently, but in a moment he sat up straighter.

"Ahh," he said. "Truly, it is magic. My head is shrinking back to its former size."

"My father, listen to me," Carlson said. "Please. I am white and I know the white man's things. For hundreds of years, for time beyond the memory of the oldest priest, the Bora-Ka have lived in their own way and have been happy and have wanted nothing. Now —"

"Now," said Halu, "the people of Bora see some of the things they have been missing. Tell me, my son, did you not say that the plans of the white men would bring many of their kind to the island?"

"Yes," said Carlson bitterly.

"And their women? The tall women with big breasts and the long, white legs?"

"Yes."

"And much of the magic liquid they call *gin?*"

"Yes," Carlson snarled.

"Then I see nothing wrong with the plans of the white men," Halu said. "Surely if they come, they will share their *gin* with us and let us borrow their women." He yawned and stretched. "Ah, the blood begins to return to my veins. Was not it a fine *lamua* last night?"

Carlson snorted.

Halu stood up, still imposingly strong and muscular, though in his mid years. "I think I shall call my paddlers and take my canoe out to the ship of the white men and talk to them more about this plan of theirs. Perhaps they will let me borrow one of their women."

"Perhaps," said Carlson bitterly.

"And because I do not speak their language, you shall also come to serve as interpreter."

Carlson stood up, shaking his head. "I don't want to go out there."

Halu's face went stern. "But you must. It is the request of the headman. And of your father-in-law."

Carlson tensed. Never, in his entire time on the island, had Halu forced him to do anything he did not want to do; never had Halu invoked his authority. He stared at the erect form of his father-in-law speculatively, wondering what further changes the next few days would bring in Halu and in the islanders. *I have got to get those people away from here,* he told himself desperately.

"All right," he said.

"Then come," said Halu. "I think my head can stand the sunlight now."

Pristine in its whiteness, the yacht rode at anchor beyond the reef. Carlson, from the prow of the canoe, just behind Halu, stared at it sourly. To him, it was a harbinger of everything he detested. Already from its white insides had flowed corruption. Farley and Marlowe had been clever in planting the seed of want, and from that seed, Carlson knew, would flower a growth that would blight paradise. Halu was lusting after gin and white women, lusting so hard that he was blinded to what he already possessed. Carlson spat into the ocean, disgustedly. It was what had happened to the Sandwich Islands, later to become the tinseled, Technicolored tourist trap called Hawaii. It was what had happened to Tahiti, where Gaugin and Stevenson had once found peace, and where movie companies now capped the bad teeth of half-breed native belles and paid them ruinous wages for performing ancient ritual dances choreographed by Hollywood. Where tin-roofed honky-tonks and padded hotel bills now flourished, where the neon sign and the transistor radio had come to stay. *Progress,* he thought sourly; that it was an old story, a very ancient one, this story of paradise corrupted, made it no less sickening to him.

Bora-Ka had slept beneath the sun of innocence, but it seemed that innocence could no longer be allowed and must be destroyed wherever it raised its head, as if it were a disease. And the death of innocence was always a heart breaking thing to behold.

Halu called to the paddlers: "Hurry. Stroke harder, and when we are on the white man's ship, I will ask them for some of the white man's *gin* for all of you." And the paddlers murmured approvingly among themselves and bent to their labor with redoubled vigor.

On board the yacht, Farley lowered his binoculars and said to Marlowe, "They're thirsty already. It's Halu in the bow. That louse Carlson is with him."

Marlowe grunted. He, too, was hung over. Moreover, he had left the island girl wildly unsatisfied last night. Without the special paraphernalia he required, there was no longer any manhood in him. Years of jading experience and the leaching away of vigor by age had left him incapable of taking a woman without the arousal of weird and brutal foreplay. Thus, Marlowe was in a no-good mood.

"He'd better not give us any more trouble," he growled.

"He will," said Farley tautly. "I know the type. If he weren't an idealist, he wouldn't be living here in the first place. You heard his song and dance the other night." He drummed his fingers on the rail. "I wish we could just arrange to turn him over to the sharks. But we can't. He's our only link between ourselves and the islanders. We've got to get him on our side."

"Offer him a bigger cut," said Marlowe. "And if he won't settle for that, the hell with him. This place will be a gold mine. I'm not going to let some draggle-tailed beachcomber stand between me and a gold mine."

"No," Farley said thoughtfully. "I don't think money will buy him." Farley had spent most of his life living on the thin edge of the underworld. He was a promoter of schemes that were not quite confidence games, but which rarely reached fruition. By an incredible stroke of luck, he had now come up with a scheme which was not only legitimate, but also obviously would be immensely profitable. He still had to pinch himself to realize that such good fortune had come to him, but he remained a realist who had lived by his keen knowledge of human character.

"Of course money will buy him," Marlowe grunted. "I never saw the man yet that money wouldn't buy."

"Not Carlson. No, not Carlson."

Marlowe stared at Farley irritably. "Then what would his price be? A woman?"

"Maybe," Farley said thoughtfully.

"Hell, the man's got three wives already."

"Yes," said Farley. He thought for a moment. "But I believe you've hit it, George. Even with the three women he's already got, I believe you've hit it." Suddenly he grinned.

"Margo," he said.

"Margo?" Marlowe swung his head around. "What are you talking about?"

"Carlson's been out here five years," Farley said quickly. "This native stuff is old hat to him by now. Don't tell me he doesn't lie awake nights dreaming about being in bed with a real American girl. And Margo — she'll do anything for money."

"That's right," a cool voice said behind him. "I'll do anything for money."

Farley and Marlowe turned. Margo stood there, lovely in a one-piece red bathing suit that was cut wildly low in front, high at the thighs and buttocks. The fabric fitted her as if it had been sprayed on.

Her eyes met Farley's levelly. "What you're suggesting is that I put the make on Carlson and con him into going along with your scheme, is that it?"

Farley grinned. "You catch on quick, Margo."

"It's the way I make my living," she said gravely. "What do you want me to do and how much is in it for me?"

"Wait a minute." Marlowe lifted an agitated hand. "Margo's my woman —"

"George," said Farley. "Do you want this thing to go through or don't you?"

Marlowe rubbed his face. "Of course I do."

"All right. You can do without Margo for a little while. I'll have Halu get you a nice little native girl. You can bring her out here and keep her on the yacht. In the meantime, Margo can turn on the steam with Carlson. When she gets him to where she can lead him around by the nose, we'll be set."

"What makes you think I can lead him around by the nose? He doesn't look the type to be led."

Farley let his eyes run up and down Margo's body. "You know all the tricks, don't you?" he murmured softly.

"Yes," she said, not looking away. "I know all of them. There were a few I didn't know before I met George. But he's filled the gaps in my education."

"Then use all the tricks," said Farley. "Get Carlson hooked on you. Hooked good and tight."

"You haven't said it yet," she told him thinly. "What's in it for me?"

"Three per cent," Farley said promptly. "A three per cent interest in the whole deal if you get Carlson on our side."

"Damn it, Lloyd." George Marlowe's voice was angry, protesting.

"Look at it this way, George," Farley said smoothly. "If we were buying Carlson with money, we'd have to up our ante that much."

"Three per cent," said Margo. "I'd want it in writing. This deal should be worth a half million a year, gross. I want three per cent of that gross."

"You'll have it. Just get Carlson on our side."

Margo nodded soberly. "I'll do my best."

"To a man who's been away from white women for five years," said Farley confidently, "your best ought to be plenty good enough."

"All right," said Marlowe thickly. "I'll go along with it. But you'd better produce results, Margo."

Halu climbed over the rail and immediately said the only English word he knew. "Gin," he said, smiling broadly. "Gin."

"Hello, chief." Farley put out a welcoming hand. "Glad to see you."

"Gin," said Halu, shaking Farley's hand vigorously.

Carlson swung over the rail behind Halu. His eyes met Margo's and he paused briefly with one leg in mid-air. The girl was stunning in that red bathing suit. Carlson felt his mouth go dry.

But, he told himself, he had not let himself be carried away by her last night, nude. He would not let himself be dazzled by her clad. Deliberately, he took his eyes from her and landed on the deck.

"Farley" he grunted. "Marlowe. Miss Neal."

"Hello, Carlson." Farley's grin was big. "I hope you're out here to tell me you've considered the proposition we made you yesterday and want to go along with it."

"I'm out here," Carlson said thinly, "because Halu craves gin."

"He shall have it," Farley said heartily.

"Yeah. I thought you'd see to that. There's something else Halu wants, too."

"Whatever Halu wants, Halu can have. The best is none too good for the noble headman of our future resort."

"Oh?" Carlson smiled wryly. "Well, Halu wants to borrow the use of a white woman."

Farley never missed a beat. "We can fix Halu up there, too. Has he met the Marlowe sisters?"

Carlson's eyes widened. He looked at Marlowe in

faint surprise. "Your daughters? You mean —"

"Listen," said Farley. "They may be George's daughters, but he knows them like a book. They'll take on anything that walks, crawls, or flies, from A is for aardvark to Z is for zebra. I'm sure they'll be delighted to fix Halu up." He turned to Marlowe. "Isn't that right George?"

If Marlowe had any fatherly feeling for his daughters, none of it showed. He said, as if discussing two strangers, "Yeah. They're a couple of nymphos, all right." He snapped a command at a nearby sailor. "Go find my daughters and tell them I want them up here."

"Aye, sir," and the sailor hurried off.

Halu turned to Carlson. "Will the white men give me gin? Will they lend me a woman?"

"The two women with golden hair," said Carlson thinly. "They're to be yours. And the gin, too."

"Ai," said Halu. "The white men are very generous. Ask them if we can do anything for them."

"Halu wants to know if he can do anything for you." Carlson snapped the words angrily.

"As a matter of fact," Farley smiled, "he can. Since woman trading seems to be the custom, George here would like to borrow one of the island women for a few nights."

Carlson made a disgusted face. He turned to Halu and relayed the message. Halu smiled broadly. "The white man must have nothing but the best. Never let it be said that anyone outmatched a man of Bora in generosity. You must let the white man have one of the three finest women on Bora — my daughters, your wives. Which should it be? I would suggest Tesai. She is the most adept, from my observation. Her mother trained her well."

"No!" The word burst forth from Carlson like an explosion. "No! I'll not turn over one of my women to these . . . these pigs!"

Halu's face darkened slowly into a frown. "That is not for you to say," he told Carlson slowly and distinctly. "That they are your women is true. But that they are my daughters is also true. And that I am headman of Bora-Ka is truer still. So when I say that we will give the white man only the finest, and that the finest is Tesai, so it shall be. Do you understand me, my son?" Without waiting for an answer, he leaned over the rail and called to the paddlers in the canoe, "Go to the village. Tell my daughter Tesai that she is to come with you to the yacht of the white men, prepared to stay for several nights."

"Damn it!" Carlson took a step toward Halu.

Halu's hand dropped to the *parang* that swung at his waist. His eyes were hard, his voice very soft. "Do not make me have to exert my authority, Carlson."

Carlson stood rigidly, his eyes locking with those of his father-in-law, and then he let out a long breath. Halu was, according to his lights, following only the custom of the island, and he was incapable of understanding Carlson's opposition. But it was one thing to lend a wife to an islander — Carlson had done that several times — and another to turn an innocent island girl over to something like George Marlowe. Carlson turned away from them in disgust and strode toward the bow of the yacht.

There he leaned on the rail, staring back toward

Bora-Ka, watching the canoe move over the reef. He said aloud a single, obscene, disgusted word. It was the first time he had used that word in five years.

A soft touch on his elbow made him turn. Margo Neal stood beside him, her eyes enormous and sympathetic. "I'm sorry," she whispered softly.

Carlson's lips curled, but he could not keep his eyes from the shadowy cleft of her bosom, plentifully revealed by the slashed neckline of the bathing suit.

"It's what I expected," he said bitterly.

"I told you to be wary of them the other night," Margo said.

Carlson frowned. "Why did you come to my room the other night?"

Margo laughed, a small sound freighted with contempt, not for him, but for herself.

"You spend months cooped up on a ship with George Marlowe," she said, "and see if you won't go anywhere to get away from him."

"Why do you stay with him?"

She shrugged. "What else is there to do?" She turned and stared toward the atoll. "I can't just hide away on an island the way you've done." After a pause, she added: "God knows, I wish I had the nerve to."

"Maybe you could," Carlson said, a new softness in his voice. "It's not really so bad, once you get used to it."

"Living in a grass hut? Eating fish day after day? No thanks." Her voice was sultry. "I'm not the type."

"What type are you?" Carlson asked softly.

"Who, me? Ohhh . . ." She pretended to think. "I'm the bright lights and jazzy music and let's dance all night type. I'm a candle-burner. Both ends at once."

"It's a habit you can kick," Carlson said. "I used to be the type myself. Remember? I was very big in armpits."

She laughed. "After armpits, I guess fish day after day can't be very bad."

"After George Marlowe," he said, "I wouldn't think it would be so bad either."

"You may have something there." She put a hand on his arm. He did not move the arm away. "Look. When you go back to the island, take me with you. I mean, just for a little while. I want to get away from these . . . creatures on this yacht. I want to see your island. See what it looks like in daytime, when I'm not drunk and — and lecherous."

"You're not lecherous now?"

"Not like I was last night. Oh, I guess I'm always a little bit lecherous. That's how I make my living." She smiled up at him, and her hand moved up and down his arm. "I want to see how a man with three wives lives. Will you take me?"

Carlson hesitated. Then he shrugged. "I guess so. If they'll let you go."

"Don't worry," said Margo. "They'll let me go."

The three sisters, Tesai, Kama, and Valu, sat in the shade of Carlson's hut, reminiscing about last night's *lamau*. "It was a very fine one," said Kama. "The white man's drink is something very good, and I wish we had more of it."

"So do I," said Valu.

"I, too," said Tesai. "But I am afraid our husband

does not approve of it. Certainly it makes one do strange things."

"I did nothing strange," said Kama. "Only what I always do. But my head was full of magic and my insides full of fire and I enjoyed it immensely, more than ever before."

"It was that way with me, also," Valu said.

The two sisters stared at the third. "Did you do something strange, Tesai?" Valu asked at last.

"Ai. It was something taught me by the white woman."

"By the white woman? And what strange thing did she reach?"

"Something," said Tesai, "beyond all experience." She told the girls briefly, succinctly, and with the flat and frank directness of the Bora people what Joyce Marlowe had done to her, and what she had done to Joyce.

The other two girls listened, wide-eyed.

"Two women? Like that? Who would have ever thought it?" Kama said at last, when Tesai's account was finished.

"It sounds very strange. I do not know whether it sounds enjoyable or not. To touch a woman like that. What is the profit in it?" Valu was frowning. But the nipples on her breasts had begun to jut.

"The only reason for it I can discern," Tesai said, "would be to satisfy one's self when a man is unavailable or too tired. But for that, it is very good."

"Then it might be of worth," said Kama. "For with three women to every man on Bora-Ka, we all know that none of us ever quite have our fill."

It is true that a man exhausts long before a woman," said, Valu. "But I still do not understand. You have told us, but I cannot see a picture in my mind of how this thing is done."

"Truly," said Tesai, "it is very simple. There is nothing to it."

"But how?"

Tesai hesitated. "If I show you, you will not laugh at me?"

"Certainly not," both sisters said immediately. Kama added: "It is a thing that might be of much value to us to know. Many are the times when it is an imposition on our husband, tired from a day's fishing, to ask him to satisfy us. If we could do it ourselves, it would be the lifting of a great burden from him, and we three would sleep much sounder at night as well. Show us, Tesai."

"All right," Tesai said. "You must lie back, Kama." The girl lay back. "Like this?"

"That is right. And you must loosen your *pareu*." Kama unfastened the cloth that bound her.

"Now what, my sister?"

Tesai straddled her sister on hands and knees. "Now I will show you," she said, and she bent her head.

Kama closed her eyes. A moment later, she gasped. "Yes," she whispered. "It is as you said . . ."

Valu watched, arms folded across her breasts, eyes wide. Her breathing came stertorously. Suddenly she reached for the fastening of her *pareu*.

"Wait a minute," she said. "I have an idea. If we all arrange ourselves thus . . ."

A half hour later, they lay exhausted. A shadow fell across them as Tekua appeared at the doorway of the hut.

"Tesai," he said. "Come with me. It is the command of your father that you be given to the short, fat white man for his use for several days."

Tesai sat up quickly. "The short fat one? That is not good. I do not like him. His eyes — they are slimy-looking, like the inside of a sea slug when it has been cut in half."

"Your father commands it."

"My husband? Does he command it too?"

Tekua hesitated. "Yes."

Tesai arose slowly. "Then so be it. If my husband commands it, I must go. Farewell, sisters."

Kama and Valu's faces were envious. "I think you're lucky," Valu said. "There will be *gin* on the ship, and you will also undoubtedly learn many new things about the white way of making love."

"You must be sure to remember them all," Kama added. "So that you can teach them to us when you return."

"Yes," said Tesai. "Of course I will."

Tekua took her arm. "Come," he said. "The canoe waits."

8

CARLSON WATCHED HALU DISAPPEAR INTO a stateroom with a bottle of gin and the two Marlowe sisters. The girls had come promptly in response to their father's summons. They displayed no shock at all when Farley had told them in crass terms what they were to do.

"Make him happy," he had said. "Make him very, very happy. When you get through with him, I want him to be forever dissatisfied with his own kind of women. I want him itching to see this island crawling with white women. Do you understand?"

Joyce and Anne looked Halu up and down speculatively. "He may be getting along in years," Anne said finally, "but he looks like he's still got what it takes. Okay. Anything for kicks."

"Yes," Joyce added. "Anything for kicks. Come along, Grandpa." She ran her hand over Halu's belly in a caressing gesture for which no interpreter was needed, then took his arm and led him down a companionway.

Carlson watched grimly. Beside him, Margo Neal said: "He's getting in over his depth. I feel sorry for him."

Carlson looked at her. "I feel sorry for us all," he said tautly.

Farley came up to him, that oily grin still on his face. "The old man takes to civilization very well, don't you think, Carlson?"

"Yes," Carlson said tersely.

Farley's grin faded; his face became sober, and he put a hand on Carlson's arm. "Look friend," he murmured, "why fight it? If you go along with us, you'll be a rich man. You can go back to the States and live like a king. Or you can stay on out here and still live like one. Hell, you can't fool me. This native stuff may be all right for the short term, but an American has got to have American women sooner or later." His glance flicked to Margo. "How can you compare a woman like Margo here to one of those little daughters of nature of yours?"

Carlson said, very quietly, "Farley, I told you yesterday I wasn't interested in your proposition. Bora-Ka may be the last place left on earth where people like you haven't managed to get a foothold. There has got to be one place like that somewhere. You talk about civilization. I happen to think that there's more to civilization than neon signs and shot glasses with false bottoms and rigged slot machines. I happen to think that civilization is a state of mind. And the people here were far more civilized than you will ever be if you live to be a million — until you took that case of gin ashore last night."

"Please," Margo said quickly. "I'm tired of hearing all these philosophical arguments. Lloyd, I'm going ashore with Mr. Carlson. He's promised to show me the island. Square it with George, will you?"

Farley nodded. "I think it's a fair trade. After all, George will have a native girl to keep him company. I'm sure there'll be no objection." His eyes flickered out to sea. "Here comes the canoe back now. I'll have one of the men get some gin for the paddlers."

He moved away before Carlson could object. Then Carlson went to the rail and watched the canoe approach, moving smoothly as the bronzed paddlers stroked with sure, strong motions. In the prow, he saw Tesai sitting a little tensely, and he muttered a curse under his breath.

The canoe came alongside, and Tesai, escorted by Tekua, ascended the ladder. As she came over the rail, breasts heaving with the exertion of the climb, she smiled at Carlson. "My husband. I understand you have loaned me to the short, fat white man. I will do my best to make him happy." Then she looked at Margo. "Have you borrowed the white woman again?"

Carlson said crisply, "No, I am not borrowing her. She just wanted to see the island and I will show it to her."

"She is very beautiful and her breasts are magnificent. Maybe she should take my place in your hut until I return."

"No," Carlson said quickly. "No, there'll be nothing like that. Tesai, if the white man does anything to harm you, let me know."

Tesai looked confused. "Why should the white man want to harm me?"

"Never mind." At that moment, George Marlowe came up, his little red eyes probing at Tesai's half-nude, bronze figure, still glittering with a beading of sea-spray from the canoe trip. Carlson saw something glow deep in those little animal eyes as Marlowe took in the innocent, trusting face, the out-thrust breasts, the smooth curve of stomach and hip disappearing into the fabric of the *pareu*, the shapely calves and bare feet revealed below the hem of the garment.

"Well," Marlowe grunted, "this should prove interesting." He put out a hand and squeezed one of Tesai's breasts without gentleness. "Nice," he said, "real nice." Margo Neal looked away quickly, an expression of anguish on her face.

Farley approached. "I've passed out gin to all your paddlers. Carlson, I hope you'll take this with our compliments. Maybe it will soften your attitude." He handed Carlson an unopened bottle of very good Scotch.

Carlson took it reluctantly. "Thanks," he said harshly. "I'll drink it — but it won't change my mind a bit." He glanced at the canoe riding alongside the yacht. "Come on, Margo. The paddlers are waiting. Tesai, remember what I said. Let me know if anything happens to you which you are reluctant to endure." The last was in the island dialect.

"So this is how you've been living," Margo said, a half hour later as they strolled along the aisle between the two rows of huts nestled in the coconut grove. "It all looks very peaceful, very quiet."

"It has been," Carlson said, "until now. Here, this hut is mine." He let her into one of the open-front structures of reeds and grass and palm fronds.

"How primitively you have lived," Margo said, her eyes sweeping around the hut. "Only reed mats to sleep on. A few pots in which to cook. A wooden pillow. Do you really like living this way?"

"There's nothing wrong with life once it's stripped down to the essentials," Carlson said. "It's only the non-essentials that botch things up and cause the trouble. After one gets used to it, a reed mat is as comfortable as a mattress, a wooden pillow as good as a down one. The things one can't get used to are dishonesty and libertinism. They didn't exist on the island — until now."

Margo put her hand on his arm. "Don't be so bitter. Your view is as one-sided as Farley's and Marlowe's. You can't hide from life. You can't dig a hole and pull the hole in after you. Don't you know that life always catches up with you?"

"Let's skip it," said Carlson.

"All right. I think that's a good idea. Where are your other two wives?"

"They must be down at the beach, swimming."

"Three devoted wives," Margo said musingly. "You are a very fortunate man."

·"No more fortunate than the other Bora men."

Margo looked preoccupied. She went on, as if talking to herself. "Everything reduced to the bare essentials. Food, shelter, and sex."

"You forgot one thing."

"What's that?"

Carlson looked at her. "Love," he said.

Margo laughed harshly. "I'd almost forgotten there was such a thing."

"You don't sound as if you've had much experience with it."

"I haven't," she said promptly, and she took his arm. "Come on. Show me the rest of the island."

They made the steep climb to the top of the plateau. Margo was panting slightly when they came over the rim, her deep breathing pushing her breasts against and out of the low-slashed neckline of the red bathing suit she still wore.

"This is the highest part of the island," said Carlson. "Here's where they want to put the air strip."

Margo looked at the long, smooth expanse of grass, rimmed at the edges with the lush greenery of tropical growth. From this high eminence, she could see the limitless blue stretch of sea and sky beyond the island. She could see the coral knobs that were the other islands of the atoll gleaming whitely in the sunlight. "It's very lovely," she said.

"I think so," Carlson murmured.

"What's on the other side of this rise?"

"There's a little waterfall, with a pool below it. The Bora people call it the place of shining water.

There's natural water in the structure of the island, and it springs out of the side of this plateau and runs off."

"I'd like to see it," Margo said.

"It's only a short walk." Carlson took her arm and they crossed the plateau.

As he walked beside her, he was aware of a curious turmoil within him. There was no denying that it was good to be able to talk in English, and to express thoughts more complicated than the necessity for catching more fish or making love. Once he had been a man who had enjoyed conversation and the company of glamourous women. No matter how beautiful the women of Bora-Ka were, they lacked that glamour, that highly-polished sheen, that only the women of American knew how to achieve. Until now he had not realized just how much he had given up to gain what he had.

He watched her move ahead of him down the path on the other side of the plateau, graceful, lovely; the tight fabric of the bathing suit limning every rounded curve, hugging the swaying, opulent breasts, the full half-moons of her buttocks. He remembered the passion with which she had met him that night on the yacht, and, unable to take his eyes from the long-legged beauty of her, he felt the sharp, involuntary thrust of desire. He wanted her.

Then he heard her gasp of admiration. The path ended on level ground, where a wide, blue pool lay in a glade amidst the tropical foliage. It was fed by a silver waterfall plummeting perhaps fifty feet, springing full-blown out of the side of the plateau. "What a beautiful spot," he heard her whisper.

He came up beside her. "I didn't know there was a

place this quiet, this lovely, this peaceful in the whole world," she went on, her face intense.

Carlson's voice was harsh. "Take a good look at it. If your friends have their way, two years from now it'll be littered with empty beer cans and sandwich wrappers, crawling with fat-legged old women in abominable bathing suits and skinny old men in baggy shorts."

"No!" she exclaimed. "No, that shouldn't happen!"

"I guess there's no help for it," Carlson said. "It's progress."

She turned to him. "And if it happens, what will you do?"

"I'll move on. Somewhere in the Pacific, there must be another island. Maybe not like this. But maybe enough like this so a man can live in peace."

"I see." Suddenly her grave face relaxed. "Let's not ruin the way it is now by talking about the way it will be. I want to swim in that pool."

"Go ahead," Carlson said.

"Will you join me?"

"Yes."

His eyes widened sightly as she reached behind her and unzipped the bathing suit. "One should wear nothing to swim in a place like this," she said. She peeled down the suit, standing before him unashamed. He watched her huge breasts spring free of the built-in bra; their white bulk quivering as if glad to be released, their nipples, large and pink, protruding a good half-inch. She slipped the suit down over her waist and past the curve of hips and then she was naked. That flare of desire in Carlson blazed higher; he made a sound in his throat and stepped toward her.

Quickly, gracefully, she eluded him and, in an arching dive, plunged into the water of the pool. She disappeared and then reappeared, floating on her back, her breasts projecting like twin conning towers. Carlson was hardly aware that he was stepping out of his own single garment, then he dived after her.

She laughed and swam away. She was a good swimmer, moving with clean, easy strokes. She headed for the bottom of the cascading waterfall, where it churned the pool at the bottom of the cliff. Carlson, like a seal in the water, glided after her.

The waterfall made thunder in their ears as he caught her. Her hair hung wetly over her face. She laughed at him, great, dark eyes dancing, as he seized her and pulled her around. He felt the teasing touch of her breasts against his chest under the water, of her thighs locking him for a moment. Then she had wrenched loose and was swimming away again, heading for the bank this time.

She was out of the water and on the edge of the ferny shore when Carlson climbed out. She stood there laughing, breasts rising and falling with the impetus of her mirth. Carlson thought that she was very beautiful, and he seemed to view her through a fog that he knew was the swirling mists of his own desire.

As she looked him in the face, her laughter died, her expression became serious. He saw her lips part, saw the white teeth and the pink, flowing motion of the tongue lurking behind them. Then she said the single word: "Carlson," and she opened her arms to him.

He grabbed her savagely, pulling that soft, white, cool, wet body tightly against him. His mouth crushed down on hers, and he felt the immediate thrusting response of her tongue. His hand swept down the smoothness of her back, seizing and cupping one heavy buttock. She rotated her body against his, moving breasts and hips in a circular motion, and Carlson's response was immediate. He felt her hand going down his back, over his buttocks, seeking and finding, and suddenly she dropped to her knees.

Carlson stood tautly, eyes closed, his hands behind her head. She was very adept, very practiced at what she was doing.

"Wait," Carlson said at last; "wait." But she was so lost in passion herself that she did not hear him. Carlson pushed her head away. She whimpered slightly and sank to the ground, buttocks rising and falling, legs twisting pleadingly.

Carlson dropped, his lips seeking her breasts, his tongue tracing over and around them, his mouth doing things to the hard, sharp points; her whimpering increased in cadence. It was like the whining of a starved puppy. Her legs locked themselves around him and drew him downward, her body arched itself to meet him, and her arms locked around his neck.

Carlson buried his face in the soft, overflowing flesh of her breasts and moved forward, and almost instantly a shuddering spasm racked her. It was as if he had set off a chain explosion in her; they came again and again, and each had its cumulative effect on him. He moved against her harder and harder, caught up in an insane desire to drive himself ever further, impossibly further, and he felt a tremendous boiling in himself, a shrieking for release. Then another one of those spasms shook her, greater than all the rest, and her body became a thing with a life of its own, drawing him in, thrusting him, drawing him back, and Carlson was lost completely in the passion-fog that blinded him. He felt as if he were falling apart — there was a moment of overwhelming ecstasy. Margo shrieked; it was a thin piercing sound, and her legs were like iron and her body stayed high off the ground, except for the bearing points of her shoulders, and her weight hung from Carlson, her nails digging into the back of his neck, her mouth clamped tight on the ridge of his shoulder. Carlson shuddered all over, and Margo shrieked again and then gasped, and suddenly the fog was lifting and they were dropping together, completely spent, to the softness of the fern-clad round.

They lay without speaking. Margo's eyes were closed; her arms and legs still held his body tightly against hers, and even if he had wanted to disengage, he would not have been able to.

But he did not want to. The clean, soft, perfumed warmth of her body against his was too good to relinquish. He nibbled at the flesh around his lips.

Suddenly she said something that surprised him. "It's stopped."

He lifted his head lackadaisically. "What's stopped?"

"The howling."

"What?"

"Inside of me, for a long time, there's been something howling. Something that I have never been able to quiet. It's stopped now."

Carlson let out a long breath. He was not certain what she meant. "Everything stopped inside of me for a little while," he murmured, and then he dropped his lips to her breasts again. He moved his body. "But it's beginning to start again now..."

On board the yacht, George Marlowe closed the stateroom door behind him and stood looking at Tesai, who was marveling at the strangeness of the furniture, the opulence of this, Marlowe's private retreat.

Wonderingly, she raised her head and looked at Marlowe. He was not, she thought, an appetizing man to have to spend the night with. She was used to the iron-muscled leanness of the men of the island, used to bodies kept to the peak of muscular perfection by the hard exercise of paddling and swimming, fishing and diving and the conquest of the high coconut palms. Truly, this short and blubbery white man with the slimy eyes was of another breed. Nevertheless, her husband and her father had commanded her to do his bidding, and their commands were law. Doubtlessly, they would have not turned her over to him unless they were sure that he would use her well. Nevertheless, she could not quench her instinctive repulsion. Perhaps, she thought, some of the white man's *gin* would make things better, for truly it could do magical things. So she said the word hopefully.

Marlowe's puffy lips curved. "Gin? Sure, you can have all the gin you want." He went to a cabinet, took out a glass, put some ice in it, and poured it nearly full of straight gin.

Tesai marveled. She touched the ice and took her finger away quickly. It was something she had never seen, never even imagined, before. It was very cold, like the greatest depths of the ocean, when one had dived farther than ever before. Would it, she wondered, change the effects of the magical liquid? She took a hesitant sip.

Actually, she found to her relief, it made the *gin* easier to drink. It seemed to kill some of the raw, harsh, pungency of it that was always a block at first. She drank a long, deep drink, while Marlowe watched, grinning crookedly.

"Not too much at one time," he said. "You'll pass out."

Tesai did not understand the words, but she caught his meaning. Obediently she put the glass aside and waited for the first drink to dig its clawing fingers into her sensibilities. It did that quickly, and almost immediately, through a fog that seemed to begin to veil her eyes, the white man looked much better. Ai, he was a man, and one of the magical properties of the drink was that it made one want a man incessantly and with a great, deep longing.

With an instinctive seductiveness, she unfastened the garment she wore about her waist and stepped out of it. She was pleased by the fire that lighted itself in the man's slimy eyes as they ran up and down her naked body. That was a point of pride with Tesai; she had the universal feminine determination that no man, no matter how undesirable, should be allowed to remain really insensitive to her charms.

She put her hands under the bronze globes of her breasts and lifted them, smiling at Marlowe. Deliberately, she moved her legs and made a motion with her hips, a clear invitation for him to take her quickly and directly and lustily, in the fashion of the island men.

To her surprise, he did not respond immediately.

He was sweating profusely and she saw his thick tongue run across his lips, but instead of going to her and touching her, he turned back to the cabinet where the *gin* was kept and made himself a drink comparable to hers, though of a different colored liquid.

A little miffed, Tesai took another swallow of her own drink. The wanting of a man was a wild clamor within her now. She pointed at a crucial spot of her body, trying to make clear to him exactly what she felt.

He grinned and said something that she did not understand. Then he began to take off his own clothes.

Ai, she thought, it was very good that she had drunk what she had drunk and wanted what she wanted so badly. Otherwise, she would have laughed at him and run away from him fleetingly. That bulging belly, fish-belly white. . .

She drank again, making more wanton gestures. She walked to Marlowe and pressed herself against him. Still he seemed not to be responding. Her eyes told her easily that he was not yet stirred, and she wondered at it. Instead of clutching at her, he turned away from her and went to a lazaret built into the wall.

He took something from it and turned back to her. What he held puzzled her; steel ringlets linked by chain. He laid them on the table and pulled her arms behind her, wrists together. Before she could wonder at this, she felt the cold snap of the cuffs as they closed over her wrists. She tried to pull her hands out before her, but they were held tightly.

"Wait," she said in her own dialect. "Stop. I do not like this."

But the white man paid no attention to her voice.

Instead, he pushed her, and, off balance, she fell back on the bunk.

She did not like what she saw in his eyes as they played over the nude, bronze length of her. She tried to rise, and he pushed her back. Suddenly afraid, she open her mouth to scream. A wooden gag shut off the first syllable of sound; before it could emerge, he locked it quickly in place with a leather strap.

Tesai twisted and writhed on the bed, terrified now, seeing that the white man was beginning to be aroused at last, seeing the glittering animal expression of lust in his little eyes. He held up some more of the steel things. Before she could elude him, he had locked one around an ankle and fastened it to a bedpost, then he did the same with the other foot. Tesai suddenly found herself stretched out and helpless on the bed, and now the white man was very, very excited.

He went back to the lazaret, and when he returned, he had in his hand a broad, leather strap. Tesai screamed behind the gag, soundlessly, as he raised it. Then it slapped down across her unprotected breasts with terrific impact, and her whole body shivered and rippled with pain. She made those soundless screams again and again as he hit her over and over, the strap missing no tender and exposed part of her, driving her insane with agony such as she had never before experienced. And with each blow, the white man seemed to become more and more frantic.

And as he hit her again and again, Tesai at last stopped screaming. She lay inertly in a fog of pain and drunkenness and desire, absolutely unable to tell where one left off and the other began.

And at last the white man was ready, and finished with the strap, and, with a wild motion, he at last flung it aside. Tesai felt the bed give as his weight was added to it, then he was throwing himself down on her chained, helpless, and unprotected body, and his slavering face loomed above hers, and it was simultaneously one of the worst things she had ever experienced and strangely one of the best.

9

DAZED AND ALMOST STAGGERING, HALU, THE
the headman, emerged from the stateroom
where he had been sequestered with the two
Marlowe girls. The sisters followed him, re-
arranging their scanty attire.

Lloyd Farley looked at the ludicrous figure the
drunken and exhausted islander made and grinned. "Well,
girls, did you take care of him properly?"

Joyce Marlowe laughed shortly. "Ha. He won't be
any good for those wives of his for a week."

Farley addressed Halu. "Chief, did you have fun?"

Halu smiled foolishly, understanding the gist of the question and nodding his head vigorously. Affectionately, he threw his arms around the two blonde girls, one hand cupping a breast of each.

"I would like to buy these two for wives," he said in the island dialect.

Farley, of course, did not understand. He said: "If you need more gin, there's plenty of it."

Halu caught a single word and and brightened. "*Gin?*" He nodded his head.

Farley gestured to the stateroom. "Take him back in there and tank him up again."

"But he's not any good any more," Joyce complained, as if being told to accept a broken Christmas present.

"Don't underestimate these islanders," Farley said. "He'll be fit to fight again after a little rest. You girls know a lot of tricks. Use them on him. I don't want him to miss a thing."

They grumbled, but obediently they pushed Halu back into the stateroom and closed the door. Farley grinned and turned to the rain, looking speculatively at the island in the distance.

I wonder how Margo's making out? he thought. His grin widened. *Lloyd,* he told himself, *you have hit the jackpot at last. All these years of living on the ragged fringe. . . . they're behind you now. You always knew were going to strike it rich some day, and that day's come.*

His chest swelled with pride as he thought how adroitly he had arranged things, how well he had used the tools that lay at hand. All right, so in this part of the world money meant nothing. But lust was a universal emotion, sex a tender that was legal anywhere. And though there was no way to buy the islanders' cooperation — or Carlson's — with money, sex and whiskey made a very neat substitute.

Let Halu get hooked on white women, he thought. Let Carlson get hooked on Margo. Let Marlowe have his native girl to keep him happy — and let them one and all get hooked on gin. . . In his mind's eye, he could already see the glittering glass facade of the hotel they would build. He could see the lumbering, ungainly, and lucrative shapes of tourists as out of place in their bikinis and grass skirts as so many cows would have been, dotting that clean, deserted beach that shimmered yonder in the sun. The green of the palms in the distance seemed to him to match the hue of currency. An eagerness almost painful rose within him. His mind raced on beyond their immediate project. He would have only a comparatively small cut of the operation to begin with; enough to make him rich, true, but trifling in comparison with what Marlowe would own. But as Marlowe got older and more sodden with perversions, he would become progressively easier to handle as those perversions were catered to — and he, Farley, would see that they were. Some day, when Marlowe was senile, there would be a chance for Farley to make a grab, freeze Marlowe out and come up sole owner of the enterprise. His mouth almost drooled at the thought, and he began to pace the ship's deck excitedly.

He was so lost in his grandiose dreams and his self-congratulation for the way in which he had used sex to make their fulfillment possible that he nearly bumped into Captain Watts.

Jericho Watts had been a sea-going man all his life, and he was the best. Marlowe wanted nothing but the best and would not settle for less. Farley was aware that Watts's New England heritage made him view with Puritanical distress what went on aboard this ship, but he was also aware that the same New England heritage had given Watts an appreciation for the dollar which would have made renouncing his lucrative post as the ship's captain almost as sinful as being an accessory to the distressing things that sometimes occurred aboard.

"Oh, excuse me, Captain," Farley said, backing off a pace.

Captain Watts looked at him dourly, but his voice was respectful. "Sorry, Mr. Farley. I was just on my way to see Mr. Marlowe."

Farley grinned. "Mr. Marlowe can't be disturbed right now, Captain Watts."

"But —" the hawk-faced, weather-burned Watts protested.

"But nothing. Not under any circumstances. He has one of those little island flowers in his room, and I'm sure he would be enraged if he were interrupted." He gave Watts a we're-all-men-of-the-world nudge, and the captain looked pained.

"Tell me, instead, Captain," Farley suggested.

Watts sighed. "Very well, Mr. Farley. But I'd suggest you pass it on to Mr. Marlowe as soon as possible." Watts glanced at a slip of paper in his hand. "I'm afraid we're in for some heavy weather."

Farley blinked. "Heavy weather?"

"Yes. We've just picked up a weather warning relayed from Guam. Seems there's a typhoon stirring around north of us. To be on the safe side, I'd suggest we make for port."

"It's not likely to bother us, really, now, is it, Captain?"

Watts looked hesitant. "No, not on its present bearings. This is not a typhoon belt, here. Usually those things boil from east to west and it will likely miss us. Still, you never can tell. These tropical hurricanes are sneaky, and they can change course with startling speed. If it should take a notion to head in our direction, we'd be hard-put to outrun it to a suitable port."

"You're the head sailor, Captain," Farley said amiably enough, "and you know your business. But I hardly think we'll get all excited about the typhoon at this stage of the game. We've got a rather important thing going here, a business deal that may mean, in the long run, millions, and it's reaching it's climax very soon — possibly within the next forty-eight hours. We're not likely to be blown away by then, are we?"

"Let's hope not," said Watts tersely. "But my recommendation still stands. We can't get across the reef into that lagoon; we draw too much water, and we're a sitting duck for any big wind that comes along out here. It wouldn't take minutes for us to be knocked up on the reef and driven aground and broken up."

"You're a person who looks on the dark side, Captain Watts. You have a very negative attitude."

Watts's gaze was a trifle contemptuous. "I'm a sailor Mr. Farley. I carry the responsibility for this ship. It's not one I take lightly."

"Neither is the responsibility of interfering with a

million-dollar deal one you should take lightly."

Watts shrugged and sighed. He handed Farley the slip of paper. "I suggest you give this to Mr. Marlowe as soon as he's free, nevertheless."

"Oh, by all means," said Farley. "Trust me, Captain Watts." He took the slip of paper and put it in his shirt pocket.

Watts said tersely: "Thank you, Mr. Farley," and turned on his heel and strode away. Farley, grinning crookedly, watched him go. When the Captain had rounded a corner, Farley took the slip of paper from his pocket and glanced at it briefly. It was the text of a weather message.

Much of its technical data made little sense to Farley, but he was fairly sure that there was nothing contained in it that represented any immediate danger. He walked to the rail and stared at the island again. Once more, the palm trees looked like currency to him. He grinned sardonically and tore the slip of paper into tiny bits and watched the little ragged pieces of it flutter down the white side of the ship to land like snowflakes in the warm, blue water below.

It was late in the afternoon when Carlson and Margo came down the path from the plateau and into the village. They had walked slowly from the pool, hand in hand, foolishly like two children deep in puppy love.

Margo was silent and thoughtful. It was strange, very strange. As long as Carlson held her hand like that, the wild, inchoate howling within her remained mute. She somehow felt, in the big man's touch, all the love and security that she had missed for so long and hungered for so much.

And, she thought bitterly, *it is my job to betray him*.

She closed her eyes tightly and instinctively squeezed his hand. There was no doubt that he was beginning to be in love with her. She knew enough about men to be able to tell that. And there was no doubt that she loved him.

And so I must betray him, she thought. It was, she told herself, absolutely necessary that she betray him, for it was the only way that she could have him permanently. As long as the island remained unspoiled, he would not leave it. But even if he wanted her to, she could not live on it while it remained so primitive. She had to have the adjuncts and comforts of civilization; she could not squat half-naked over a flickering fire and be content eating half-cooked fish.

But if she could convince him to let the two men on the yacht have their way, the island would become civilized enough to be bearable for her. And she could live on it — with Carlson. So it was as much to her interest as to anyone's — the three per cent cut aside — to see the project go through. If it didn't, she and Carlson would be separated as surely as the tide that carried the yacht ebbed out to sea.

"You're awfully quiet," Carlson said, breaking the long silence.

"Yes." She squeezed his hand again. "I was just thinking that you are not like any man I ever met before."

"That's odd," he said. "Because I was just thinking that you're not like any woman I've ever known. You're aware, sophisticated, maybe even a little hardboiled. But somehow I think you appreciate this island and the way it is. I couldn't imagine any white woman ever doing that. Not without a lot of shiny tinfoil to amuse and attract her, the way kids are attracted by gimcrack toys."

"You don't think much of American women, do you?"

"I didn't, until now. My — my wife back in the States wasn't a very attractive representative of the breed. Frigid, yet selfish, all take, no give, greedy and indifferent to anything that couldn't be banked, worn or ridden in. But somehow I feel that you're different."

Margo took in a long breath. "I would hate to say I was."

"I'd hate to think you weren't."

Suddenly he halted tilted his head as if listening. Margo looked at him. "What's the matter?"

"Don't you hear it?"

She strained her hearing senses. Then she nodded. It was burst after burst of shrill, high-pitched giggling and whooping coming from the village, which lay only a short distance ahead of them.

"It sounds like your friends are very happy," she said.

Carlson's mouth tightened. "It sounds like my friends are very drunk," he snapped. "Come on." Still holding her hand, he hurried forward.

When they emerged into the village street, they saw that it was deserted. The choruses of drunken laughter and yells were coming from the individual huts. Since they were all open-fronted, there was no difficulty in determining their origin.

The huge supply of gin Farley and Marlowe had sent back with the paddlers had been distributed and was doing its work well. So, too, were the seeds of sensuality planted by what Joyce Marlowe had done first to Tekua and then to Tesai. Normally, at this time of the day, the islanders would have been busy. Their canoes would have been beyond the reef, fishing. The women would have been actively preparing the evening meal for the fishermen's return. But nobody seemed to be attending to business at all right now. Instead, there were dozens of separate orgies taking place.

Carlson and Margo stared incredulously at the uninhibited scenes that met their eyes in the various huts. The one man and the three women who, on the average, inhabited each hut were, in all of them, exhibiting great ingenuity in putting into drunken use the lessons in lust that they had learned. Surely these things were delightful novelties that the whites had made them aware of and must be tested to the utmost! While their children watched wide-eyed and curious, in some cases imitating the adults, the islanders of Bora-Ka were deep in gin and complicated love.

Carlson made a sound of disgust low in his throat. Margo stared at one foursome, all linked together in incredible fashion, a single man, three women. "Your people learn fast," she whispered.

"They had good teachers," Carlson grated. "Fine, accomplished, depraved teachers." He stalked down the street until he came to his own hut.

Kama had passed out from too much gin. Valu lay athwart her, barely able to move. She was nuzzling Kama's inert body desperately and whimpering with unsatisfied desire. As Carlson's shadow darkened the doorway, Valu rolled away from her sister and sat up, mouth gaping open in a foolish grin. "Ai, my husband, you are home, thanks be. And the white woman too, and that is good. We shall have much delight. Come in come in, there is plenty of gin for all, thanks to the generosity of those on the yacht." She crawled across the hut on hands and knees, tongue lolling, breasts hanging, and clawed at Carlson's bare legs. She got to her knees and buried her face hungrily against his body. As he stepped back, she fell forward on the sand. She whimpered and half arose again, this time clawing at Margo. "You," she whimpered in the dialect. "Then will you not do to me what the white women do?"

Carlson's slap spun Valu's head around and knocked her backward across the hut. She landed on her buttocks, legs sprawling. Carlson saw tears ooze from her eyes. But she did not move, and in a moment, she was giggling foolishly. She swabbed the tears away with the back of her hand and reached for the gin bottle. She took a long drink of it, sighed, and put it aside carefully. Then she grinned at Carlson.

"If nobody else will make me happy," she blurred, "I will delight myself." Her hand moved down her belly.

Carlson took Margo and spun her away. "You see," he grated, his voice trembling with rage. "They can't handle the stuff. One drink does to them what a whole bottle would to a white man."

"I'm sorry," Margo whispered. "But . . . do you mean to tell me all this was unknown among the islanders until we got here?"

Carlson nodded, his face a mask of fury. "Their

concept of love was simple, innocent, and straightforward. It had to be. If it weren't, a man with three wives would soon have found them in competition with each other to see who could perform the most outrageous things. There would have been family jealousy instead of family harmony and the whole family structure would have fallen apart. I guess that's what has happened to it now." He looked down at his hand curiously. "I never hit one of my wives before," he murmured almost incredulously. "I — I never had to."

Then he was striding angrily toward the side of the beach that flanked the lagoon. "Come on," he said fiercely. "Let's get away from all that. I don't want to see it." He seemed to think for a moment. "I don't believe it's even the variations in love that have shocked me. It's the speed with which they've learned all that — that's what sickens me. Thinking how quickly they'll learn all the things that are really bad. The value of money and greed for what it will buy. The concept of possessiveness and the corresponding concept of unfaithfulness and adultery. You people have opened a whole Pandora's box here."

They had reached the beach now. Margo stood quietly, chastened, looking out over the reach of blue water to the other, smaller islands. Then she clasped Carlson's arm. "There's one man who hasn't been led astray."

Net over his shoulder, an island man was slogging through the surf toward them. In the dying rays of the sun, his gray hair shone silver.

Carlson nodded. "Danakau. One of the village priests. He's a very level-headed, a real wise man." He held up his hand and said in dialect: "Danakau, greetings. Have you caught many fish?"

The old man's lined but handsome face was hard and set. "I fished only to get away from the abomination in the village. The white man's ways are not our ways, and surely there will be punishment." He threw his empty net on the sand. "I warned them, but they would not listen. Now it is already beginning."

"What's beginning?" asked Carlson.

Danakau gestured. "The fish have left the lagoon."

"What is he saying?" Margo asked.

Carlson's brow was furrowed. "He says the fish have left the lagoon." Switching back to the dialect: "Have you caught nothing, Danakau?"

"Nothing," said the priest tersely. "The gods of the ocean are already angered."

"So the fish left the lagoon," Margo said. "What does that mean?"

"It could mean a lot," Carlson murmured. "Normally, this lagoon is swarming with fish. All one has to do is throw in a net and pull it out again. But now Danakau has fished and not caught a single thing."

"So?"

"So the fish have gone out to deep water."

"Forgive me," said Margo, a trace of acerbity in her voice, "but I haven't had much practice at being a child of nature. What does the fact that fish get tired of one place and go somewhere else mean?"

"Bad weather," said Carlson.

"Oh. Is it going to rain?" Margo's eyes searched the sky. It was absolutely cloudless, the burgeoning sunset beginning to spread its molten glory.

"More than that," said Carlson. "There'll be a blow. A bad blow."

Margo snorted daintily. "Don't be absurd. How could fish know that in advance?"

Carlson shrugged. "You'll have to ask the fish. All I know is that in the five years I've been here, it's a sign that hasn't failed yet." Lapsing into dialect, he said: "You had better go and warn the people, Danakau."

Danakau's mouth twisted. "Warn them? The people of Bora-Ka will not listen. They are too lost in doing fantastic things with each other's bodies and drinking the magical drink of the white man. How can one warn those who are deaf?"

Carlson half turned, his eyes sweeping out across the water. Dying sunlight gilded the magnificent lines of the yacht beyond the reef. "They should be warned, too," he murmured. He turned to Margo. "I'll find some paddlers to take you back to the ship, even if I have to slap them sober."

Her hand moved down his arm. "Don't bother."

Carlson stared at her. "What?"

"I said, don't bother." She moved her body closer to his. "I think I would like to spend the night here. See how the other half lives, and what it is like to sleep on a reed mat with a wooden pillow."

"You won't like it," said Carlson.

"How do you know I won't?" Her huge, dark eyes looked directly into his. He saw her breasts heave, their slopes bulging temptingly out of the top of the bathing suit. "Please let me stay. Then we can go out and warn the yacht in the morning."

Carlson stood rigidly, staring down into her eyes.

"All right," he said at last. "You can stay."

They went back to Carlson's hut. Carlson scraped up the coals of a fire and roasted some dried fish. There was also boiled taro left from the morning. Both inert with drunkenness, Kama and Valu slumbered, snoring noisily, in the corner of the hut, bodies piled one on top of another. Carlson and Margo were, for all practical purposes, alone.

Carlson watched with amusement the expressions on Margo's face as she struggled to down the native food. But when she had eaten all she could take, she said bravely: "It's not really so bad, is it?"

"Well, it's not *haute cuisine,* either," Carlson grunted, feeling admiration for the courage she had displayed. "It does take on a certain monotony after a while. I'll be honest and admit there are times when I feel like I'd sell my soul for a plain old piece of apple pie."

"Then why fight it?" Margo asked earnestly. "Why not let Marlowe and Farley develop the island the way they want to and enjoy the best of both worlds? You can't shut your eyes to civilization forever, Rod. You were born a civilized man and lived as one most of your life. You can't just renounce all that and go back to the cave." Her voice became more intense, dropping huskily. "Rod, just imagine. If this island were developed, you could have your beach and your ocean and you could have everything else a civilized man demands as well."

Carlson's mouth twisted. "And I could watch my friends turned into beachboys — male prostitutes. And see their wives turned into female prostitutes and kootch dancers and strippers in night clubs. And watch the sewage pour out into the lagoon. No, thanks, Margo. Hell, we've talked on this subject enough." He fumbled around under some matting and brought out the bottle of Scotch Farley had given him and found a couple of coconut shell drinking vessels. "Let's have a drink. Maybe it'll take the taste of the dried fish out of your mouth." His eyes shuttled to the slumbering, interlocked bodies of his wives. "Everybody else on Bora-Ka got plastered today — why should we be exceptions?" His voice was more bitter than Margo had ever imagined it could be. He poured a huge jolt of Scotch into each of the vessels, added water from a gourd, handed her one, and lifted the other and drank long and deeply.

"Maybe a typhoon will come," he said, "and blow the damned island away and everybody's problem will be solved."

"Don't talk like that, Rod."

He drank again. "Sorry. I won't. I'm through with it for now." He lowered the vessel and looked at her across its rim. "Do you know," he whispered, "That you are the most beautiful woman I have ever seen?"

"Stop it, Rod," Margo said miserably, something hurting her deeply within.

"But you are." His voice was a trifle thick now. "There's only one thing wrong. When a Bora man and his wives sit around the hut in the evening, they wear no clothes. You've got too damned many clothes on, Margo."

"I'm not your wife," she said sharply, but she could feel the bite of the Scotch, too, feel its warmth in her insides, gentle and insidious. It gave rise to a tingling in her breasts, the return of passion. She did not look at Carlson.

"No," Carlson said slowly, after drinking again.

"No, that's true, you aren't. And you're not likely to be. I can't imagine your deciding to be wife number four in a grass hut on a godforsaken island. You're not cut out for it."

Margo drank again. "Anything any other woman can do," she said, "I can do better. Even including being wife to a beachcomber."

"Really?"

"Yes . . ."

"I doubt that," said Carlson. "I'd like to see you cleaning and drying fish."

"Well, I can."

He laughed.

"I know how to clean a fish," she said quickly. "I can do it with just two cuts. A long time ago, when I was a — a very little girl, my — my father showed me how." A burst of memory hammered against her brain, and she felt the howling begin in her once more. She drank long and deeply and held out the shell. "More," she said.

He reached for the bottle.

She smiled at him.

Carlson poured a huge dollop. He did likewise for himself. They both drank deeply, and Margo sighed. Suddenly she stood up, her eyes blazing with a strange light. She went to the two women slumbering in the corner, and she pulled the inert Valu off of the motionless Kama and dragged Valu's body into the firelight and let it drop. The firelight cast bright gleams on its bronze length.

"Look at her," Margo said harshly. "And then look at me." A little unsteadily, she began to peel away the bathing suit.

Carlson smiled.

Margo kept stripping.

She stepped out of it and threw it aside. Proudly, almost defiantly, she stood naked before Carlson. She put her hands under her breasts and lifted them in a wanton gesture. She moved her legs and tilted her hips forward.

Carlson felt his breath quicken and his throat go dry at the loveliness of her. His eyes dropped to the short, stocky, wide-hipped Kama, with her round face and small nose and coarse black hair; then traveled away and up the long, white legs and the magnificent thighs of Margo, and up the fire-gleaming ivory of her middle to the huge and shapely breasts whose ends seemed to pout redly, and beyond them to the intense, sensitive face framed by the mass of dark hair.

"Look," Maro said again. "Look and compare. Do you honestly think I would be less a wife than she? Listen, Rod Carlson, let me tell you something. I have done everything it is possible for a man and a woman to do together. I know things I could do to you that would have you shrieking with the ecstasy of them, things no other woman has ever done. If I wanted to, I could make you willing to sell all three of your wives as dogmeat for one night with me..."

Carlson half arose, making an animal sound in his throat, feeling the whiskey hot in brain and body. "Show me," he said hoarsely. "Show me..."

He reached for her, but Margo eluded him.

"Let me tell you what I can do," she taunted him. And she began to tell him, in shocking, succinct terms.

Every device and refinement of sex that she had ever learned, and they were many, she made explicit in words. "I even learned," she finished, still eluding Carlson's grasp, "to enjoy what George Marlowe did to me. I had to learn to enjoy it to bear it at all. And even if you were to use a whip on me as he did, even if that were what you liked, I would still —"

But Carlson had stopped and was standing very still his eyes wide. "What was that?"

"I said I even learned to enjoy George Marlowe's kind of sex. I —"

"About the whip," Carlson said hoarsely. "You said something about a whip."

Margo stared at him. "What's the matter? Haven't you ever heard of people like that? Sadists, who have to inflict pain before they can take pleasure? Well, let me tell you, I learned to bear the pain. I even learned to make it arouse me, to enjoy it, to look forward to it. If I hadn't, I'd have gone crazy under his whip and his shackles and his other oddball tortures —"

Carlson's teeth were showing in a snarl, and Margo's voice trailed off. "What's the matter?"

There was a great chill in Carlson, negating all the whiskey, all the lust.

"Marlowe's got one of my wives," he whispered. "Marlowe's got Tesai. . ."

Suddenly the taunting, the defiance, went out of Margo. She swallowed hard. "Then I feel sorry for her," she whispered.

"She doesn't know anything about pain," Carlson said in a voice of shock. "Why she's never even been struck by anyone's hand. And Marlowe — ?" Suddenly his body went erect, and he reached for his discarded shorts. "Get your bathing suit on," he rasped. "I'm getting some paddlers and we're going out to the yacht."

10

FARLEY WAS GETTING WORRIED ABOUT BOTH
Halu and Marlowe. Night had fallen over the
ocean, and neither of them had appeared from
his stateroom again. The two Marlowe sisters
were still locked in with Halu.

Frowning, Farley went below to the room occupied
by Halu and the Marlowe girls. He rapped on the door
peremptorily.

There was a moment's pause and then the shuffle
of bare feet across the floor. Joyce Marlowe, completely

nude, opened the door and stood there, unashamed.

Farley's eyes hardly noticed her nudity. "Where's the old man?" he asked harshly.

"Passed out again," Joyce said ruefully. "But I'll say one thing for the old buzzard, he's got real staying power." Her voice was thick, the words came hard, and Farley realized that she was quite drunk. Suddenly she reached out and grabbed him in a crass manner. "Come on in," she mumbled.

Farley pushed her hand away. Beyond her, he saw the naked Halu sprawled on a bed. Anne Marlowe, very very drunk herself, lay writhing on the floor. "Damnit," she whimpered, "come on, Joyce. We've got to pass the time somehow until he wakes up again..."

Farley said harshly: "Your sister's calling you, Joyce." He shut the door in her face and went on down the companionway.

At the door to Marlowe's room, he rapped loudly. "George? George?"

There was no answer.

Farley hammered harder. "George? Hey, George. Are you all right?"

There was a sound very much like that an animal disturbed at its feeding.

Farley's brow wrinkled.

"George? Damnit..." He slammed on the door again.

Marlowe's voice called thickly: "Go the hell away."

"But, George — You've been in there all day."

After a moment of silence, the door opened a small crack. One of Marlowe's red eyes and a strip of fishbelly white skin appeared in the crack. "Leave me alone,

Lloyd," he snarled.

Farley's frown deepened. "What in hell are you doing in there, George?"

"It's none of your concern," Marlowe whispered thickly His tongue moved across puffy lips. "But there are things I've always wanted to do, things I couldn't get away with, with Margo. I can do 'em now, with this island girl. She —"

Farley's voice was full of instant concern. "George, be careful, don't hurt her. After all, she's the headman's daughter. You don't want to ruin the deal —"

"The hell with the deal," George Marlowe snapped. "I've never had my hands on anything like this before." And the door slammed in Farley's face.

Farley turned away, countenance drained of blood. He had blundered. Oh, God, he had blundered badly. He had been aware of Marlowe's peculiarities. He should never have let Marlowe get his hands on an island girl alone like that. If Marlowe had hurt or disfigured the girl, there would be hell to pay.

His hands sweating with apprehension, Farley paced the corridor. He went back to the stateroom door, hammered again. "George. Damnit, George —"

But if Marlowe heard the summons, he paid no attention. At last Farley let out a long, whistling breath and moved away. His face was still very white when he climbed a ladder topside.

He had just made the deck, silvered with moonlight, when a voice called out from below, down at the waterline, "Ahoy the yacht."

A cold knot clinched in Farley's belly. Carlson, and if he demanded to see his wife —

A sailor hurried up. "Shall I let them aboard, Mr. Farley?"

Farley saw Margo and Carlson sitting impatiently in the canoe. "The lady and the white man," he said. "not the paddlers. Tell them to go back to the island." Then he hurried to the dining saloon.

Carlson's face was hard as he clambered over the side. He faced the knot of sailors, who were raking Margo with appreciative eyes. "You fellas," Carlson grated. "Where's Mr. Marlowe?"

"Guess he's below, sir," a seaman answered. "He's been down there all day."

Carlson was about to ask for Farley when that man's voice sounded cordially. "Ah, Carlson. Glad to have you back aboard. And Margo. Did you have a nice day ashore?"

"Where's my wife?" Carlson asked bluntly. "Where's Tesai?"

"Ah ... she's below with Mr. Marlowe." Farley put a friendly hand on Carlson's arm. "But don't worry, Carlson. She's perfectly all right. I saw her just a moment ago myself. She seemed to be enjoying herself immensely."

"I want to see her," Carlson snapped.

"Of course," Farley said affably. "I'll send word to Mr. Marlowe, and I'm sure he'll send her right up. In the meantime, come along and have a drink."

"I don't want a drink," Carlson said tautly.

"Now you're being discourteous," Farley said chidingly. "Come on, there'll be time for a short one while your wife — What's her name, Tesai?— gets herself together to come topside. Everything's already poured and waiting in the dining saloon."

"I want her here quickly," Carlson snapped.

"Don't worry, old boy, she will be. Now, wipe that scowl off your face and let's go lift a short one."

Reluctantly, Carlson followed Farley into the dining saloon, while Margo went below to her own stateroom. Farley had already poured two tall Scotches with soda and plenty of ice.

"I hope, old boy," he said, handing Carlson a glass, "that you've decided to be sensible and accept our proposition."

"Don't call me old boy," Carlson snapped. "And the answer is the same as it was this morning — hell, no."

Farley, apparently unruffled, shrugged philosophically. "Well, I'm sure you'll change your mind in time..." He raised his glass. "Cheers," he said, and drank.

Carlson also drank. He frowned and looked at Farley. There was a new tang to the Scotch. "Is this a different brand?"

"Why, no. I hope it hasn't suffered a sea change." Farley drank again, deeply. "Mine's all right."

Carlson took another swallow. "It tastes funny," he said. He blinked. Something was happening, something strange. Farley's white clad figure had begun to shimmer, as if there heat waves rising between Farley and Carlson's eyes. Carlson leaned on the table for balance. He took another swallow — this time he was certain of it. "You —" It was very hard to form words. "You push sumpin innis drink..."

Farley grinned. "Oh, don't be absurd. It's just that in five years, you've forgotten how to hold your liquor."

"No," said Carlson. The room was whirling crazily now. He dropped the glass and its contents spilled. He leaned against the table with both hands. "Damn you. Push sumpin in drink. Tryna keep me 'way from Tesai. I'll —" He tried to take a step forward.

He saw the floor hurtling up crazily to hit him.

It was the last thing he saw for a long while.

Tesai stared up with eyes blurred with pain. Her mind was no longer capable of conscious thought. What George Marlowe had done to her throughout this long, agonizing day, had destroyed her reasoning powers. She no longer had a mind; all she had were nerve endings and a body that screamed for surcease from torture and assault.

Marlowe was drunk, very drunk. He waved the straight razor around in a circle. One hand caressed Tesai's breasts.

"Zis is sumpin' I've allus wanted do," he said thickly. "Allus wanted to, never had nerve."

He lowered the razor.

Tesai screamed behind the gag. There was no sound.

"Marlowe!" Farley hammered on the stateroom door, frantically. "George. For God's sake, open up!"

From behind the door there came only an insane giggling.

Halu awakened, his head bursting with a hangover, his body drained of strength, a vague unease clawing at his entrails. Through the stateroom porthole, he saw that it was dark.

What in the name of the seagods had happened to the day? He had never lost an entire day before. What spell had the white women cast on him to make him do so now?

He swung his legs off the bed, and immediately Joyce and Anne Marlowe were on him like tigresses. "Look," Anne giggled, "he can still sit up."

"We'll fix that," Joyce mumbled. Her mouth and hands were as greedy as Anne's.

Halu blinked, and then he was filled with a sudden revulsion. There was a time for sex, but there was also a time when sex ceased to be a part of a man's life, when it was over and there were other things to go on to He stood up suddenly and ruthlessly, and the two naked girls went sprawling.

"Hey!" Joyce snapped.

Halu looked at them. "You must forgive me, white women," he said coolly. "But the time for play with women is over. My head is bursting and my body feels dried out. I have spent overmuch time in indulging myself — and it is unseemly that the headman of the Bora people should do so. What could I have been thinking of?" His words, in the fluid dialect, fell on uncomprehending ears.

Joyce and Anne clawed at him. He threw them off with even less gentleness this time. "Surely the women of the white people are like rutting sea-animals. If they bring women like this to Bora-Ka, my men will have no strength left." He strode toward the stateroom door and opened it, wrapping his loincloth about him.

His head ached excruciatingly as he climbed the ladder topside. But the cool touch of the night air helped somewhat.

There was something in the breeze, though, that registered on Halu's sensibilities immediately. He raised his head and sniffed, like a dog testing for scent; then his brow furrowed.

"Weather in the offing," he said to himself. "From out of the place where the wind gods stay. There will be danger in the rising and setting of another sun." He rubbed his face. "Ai, I have had enough of the white man's *gin* and the white man's women to last me should I live two more lifetimes! What surprising things they do to one!"

He paced the deck, making a circuit in search of Farley. "If," he said aloud to himself, "I can find the Farley white man, I shall command a boat to take myself back to shore. And also my daughter Tesai. Perhaps Carlson was right. Though it is surely very enjoyable to drink and make love in the white man's fashion, one tires of it very quickly. This is not, perhaps, a wholesome atmosphere in which to leave my daughter, and I am ashamed of myself for craving the *gin* so much that I did not think of it before and make some excuse when the white man asked to borrow her. For he does not look like a man of Bora. He looks like something spawned deep in the sea, and my daughter cannot have had a very pleasant time with him."

He heard footsteps in a corridor, and then a door opened and Farley emerged. Farley stopped short in confusion at the sight of Halu.

"Hello, chief. What brings you out? The girls run short of steam?"

"I seek my daughter, Tesai," Halu told him. Neither

understood the speech of the other, but Farley caught the word *Tesai* and Halu did not miss the expression that crossed his face.

Farley seized Halu's arm, tried to drag him back toward the stateroom he had occupied. But Halu shrugged away. "No," he said. "I have no strength left for women." And this time his meaning was plain. "Tesai," Halu went on. "Tesai, my daughter. Where is she?"

"I'll have a boat to take you back to the island," Farley said quickly, gesturing to make his meaning intelligible.

Halu shook his head. "Not without Tesai."

"Damnit," Farley said, "Tesai can't be disturbed. Tesai with big white boss. Understand?" Seeing that Halu did not, he resorted again to sign language, closing his eyes, pillowing his head. "Tesai asleep."

Halu understood this. He nodded in comprehension. "We shall go and wake Tesai up. There will be big winds by the setting of tomorrow's sun. Where is she?"

Farley was only too sure what Halu meant about waking Tesai up. He had no idea what Marlowe had done to the girl, but he feared the worst. *That damn fat animal*, he thought savagely. *Willing to see a million dollars down the drain to satisfy his own queer lusts —*

He gestured frantically. Tesai slept. Tesai would be awakened in the morning. It would be discourteous to disturb Tesai and the big white boss tonight. First thing tomorrow a boat would bring Tesai to the island. Halu had his, Farley's, promise of it.

Somehow, Farley got his meaning across. The breaking of a promise was something inconceivable to a man of Bora, and if Farley said he would do such and such a thing, there could be no doubt that such and such a thing would come to pass. Halu nodded, realizing that it was very late and that perhaps Farley was right. But in his turn, he gestured too, until he was certain that he had got across his meaning to Farley; sunrise and no later. Farley nodded agreement. Then he called to a knot of sailors, and in a few moments a boat was launched.

Halu climbed into it with grave dignity, trying not to reveal the torture that throbbed in his head. He winced only slightly as the engine roared into life and the craft shot forward over the reef, heading for the island. But he was glad when, at last, he put foot on solid shore.

He waved a dignified good-bye to the sailors, who backed water, turned the boat, and started toward the yacht. Then, anxious to talk to Carlson, he hurried as fast as the condition of his head would let him toward the village.

Halfway there, he paused at the sound of roistering. Ai, that was strange, there was no *lamua* tonight. But such giggling and laughter and whooping and shouting.

At the edge of the beach, where it merged with the coconut grove, sat a lonely, thoughtful, and almost disconsolate figure. Halu recognized it immediately. "Greetings, Danakau. Why do you sit apart thus from the merriment."

Danakau arose and looked at the chief, sourly. "So you have come back from your pursuit of *gin* and the white man's women. Do you finally give a thought to your own people?"

Halu looked down at the sand. "I am not old, Danakau. My body still has its demands and its curiosity Do
not blame me for yielding to it this once. It is cleansed
of all that now, and I return."

"Too late," Danakau said harshly.

Halu raised his head. "What do you mean?"

"I will show you what I mean." Danakau took
Halu's arm and led him through the grove to the village.
"There," he said. "That is what I mean."

Halu stared incredulously at the sight upon which
moonlight flooded.

The dozens of individual orgies that had gone on
all afternoon had flowed into the street and merged into
one. Drunken islanders rose and lurched around waving
their gin bottles and then fell back into a tangled mass
of indefatigable flesh. Halu gaped, as he saw his entire
village meshed together in unspeakable things learned
from the white women. The same unspeakable things the
white women had done to him today and which he had
enjoyed so immensely. But the sight of them now revolted
him.

Men clawed at men and women at women and the
sexes at one another, as if they were engaged in a wild
competition to see who now could plumb the greatest
depths of sensation. Even the children had been drawn
into the spree, like chips sucked into the vortex of a
whirlpool.

Halu turned away sickly.

"It is the *gin*," Danakau said. "Truly it makes them
all sick of mind."

"Yes," Halu said tautly, "it has that effect." He
spat into the sand and turned back to the nightmare

scene that filled the street.

"And you have smelled the air," said Danakau morosely. "The smell is in the air, and the fish have left the lagoon. Surely the vengeance of the gods is not slow in coming for those who forsake the ancient ways."

"I have smelled the air," Halu said. "And this," he added grimly, "has got to stop." He stood at the head of the street and bellowed at the top of his mighty lungs.

"People of Bora!" he yelled. "Listen to Halu, head man of you all!"

No one paid him the slightest attention.

He yelled louder, in a voice that could be heard above the mightiest roar of the ocean. "People of Bora! I, Halu, speak!"

A woman pulled herself out of the squirming mass of flesh that was Halu's people. She stared at Halu with drink-gazed eyes and waved a bottle of gin with an inch of liquid still in it and made a gesture of wantonness. When Halu did not respond, she dropped to her knees and soon found, hungrily, not caring to whom it belonged, another body.

Halu's lips thinned. "They will not listen," he snapped, "but an end will be put to this, nevertheless." He whirled and walked toward the shore. When he came back, he had in his hands a six-foot doubled length of palm-fiber cable, used as anchor rope by the fishermen.

Like a man incensed beyond reason, he strode among the writhing bodies on the street. Driven by every ounce of strength in his muscular arm, the rope rose and fell like a flail. There were sudden howls from those in the orgy; bodies separated, people stumbled to their feet, curious and outraged and rubbing the smarting places where the rope had done its work.

Halu marched ahead, laying about him strongly. The whack, whack of the doubled rope sounded loudly in the quiet evening, along with a chorus of pain-filled cries. When Halu reached the end of the street, the orgy was over.

Now the islanders lined the edges of the street and looked at Halu with a hangdog expression.

Halu paced up and down.

"Now," he shouted, "do not look at me like that. I have been worse than any of you. I have spent the entire day drinking the *gin* and enjoying the women of the white ship. I am no better than you. But tonight I came to my senses. So tired, so worn with my day of pleasure that I could barely stand, I stood apart from myself and looked at myself and thought; 'Is this the proper way for a man of Bora to pass a day?' We have our *lamuas*, but the whites have *lamuas* every day, and it is known by our elders that *lamuas* every day are harmful. Let the whites have them if they want, such conduct is not for the people of Bora. Now." He gestured to a place in the middle of the street. "Now the gin bottles will be brought here and emptied and if anyone retains one secretly, when it is found — and it will be, for you cannot drink the stuff without the evidence being clear in your walk and speech — he will have to deal with me. Pour!"

There was some grumbling at first, but the iron attitude of the headman and the long habit of obedience pulled the reluctant islanders forward, one by one The dregs of many gin bottles soaked into the sand, and the bottles were tossed aside.

Halu faced the hangdog islanders.

"Already there is vengence in the air for our disregard of our own customs and our adoption of the white man's customs. Tell them, Danakau."

The old priest drew himself up. "People of Bora," he called loudly. "Today the fish have left the lagoon. There is the taint of wind in the air. By tomorrow's sunset, vengeance will be upon us. Make ready. Drag all canoes to high ground. Store food and water in our refuge cave. Do all that is necessary to survive the vengeance that will certainly come."

Dozens of heads were lifted high, sniffing the air. A murmur went up from the Bora people. "Surely it is as Danakau has said."

"Disperse, then," called Halu. "Go to your huts and carry to the cave those things which you must have. Surely this will be no ordinary blow. This will be a *temaurekua*, a typhoon. Prepare for it quickly."

The people of Bora nodded. Wearily, the gin still in them, they staggered to their huts.

Kama and Valu hurried toward their father. "Our father, do not forget that our sister Tesai is on the white man's ship," Valu said worriedly. "The ship cannot survive a big wind. Tesai must be brought to shore, to the safety of the cave."

"Ai." Halu nodded. "I have already thought about her, and tomorrow when the sun comes up I shall go to the ship to get her."

11

CAPTAIN WATTS LOOKED UP FROM HIS charts, his face furrowed in a frown, and barked, "Come in!" as somebody hammered at the door of his cabin.

The radioman approached diffidently and respectfully. "Sir, another weather advisory from Guam." He held out a slip of paper.

Watts took it, said: "Thank you. I want Guam contacted every hour for advisories," and glanced at the slip of paper. He kept his face expressionless until the radioman had left. Then Watts took his cap from a hook, clapped it carefully on his head at just the right authoritarian angle, and hurried out of his cabin to find Farley.

Farley was in the dining saloon, a bottle in front of him. He had obviously been drinking heavily. His handsome face was morose, as if he had been watching something extremely valuable slip away from him. He said, not particularly cordially, "Hello, Watts. Sit down and have one."

"No, thank you." Watts held out the slip of paper. "Read that, Mr. Farley."

Farley squinted at the paper. "Hell, I can't make anything out of all this gobbledegook. What does it say?"

"It's a weather advisory from Guam. It says the typhoon has changed course. By tomorrow night we can expect to catch the outer fringe of the winds and extremely heavy seas. By sunrise tomorrow, we'll be right in the middle of it if we don't lift anchor and run before it. It's traveling at a fantastic speed, nearly our own top speed."

Farley handed the paper back to Watts. "What do you expect me to do?"

"I expect you to inform Mr. Marlowe. I want that native girl and anybody else from the island put ashore at once, and then I want to head south immediately. Maybe you've never ridden out a typhoon at sea, Mr. Farley, but I have, and I can tell you they're not much fun. This baby's a bad one. Winds of a hundred and twenty knots at the center. That's about as bad as they can get."

"It would break us up, eh?"

"Swamp us or tear us apart like an eggshell. I've seen seas sixty feet high in typhoons like this one."

Farley stood up and finished his drink. "That's just

about all we need," he said bitterly. "Captain, have you ever had something in the palm of your hand and then had it snatched away?"

"Occasionally."

"That's the story of my life," Farley grunted. "Come on, we'll go see Mr. Marlowe."

Together they went along the corridor to Marlowe's stateroom. Farley hammered at the door. "Mr. Marlowe! George!"

After a long moment's wait, Marlowe's face appeared in the crack of the door. "Damnit, what is it?"

"There's heavy weather brewing, Mr. Marlowe," Watts said respectfully. "We're going to have to haul anchor and outrun it."

The single little red eye of Marlowe focused on Watts unblinkingly. "No," Marlowe said, thickly.

"But, sir —" Watts made a frustrated gesture.

"I said no." Marlowe eased the door a crack. "Farley, you can come in. Watts, I'll talk to you later."

Watts let out a long breath. "Yes, sir." Cursing silently, his face grim, he whirled and strode away along the corridor.

When Farley had entered the stateroom, Marlowe shut the door quickly behind him and locked it. Marlowe's lips were trembling slightly. "Lloyd, I gotta have your help."

Farley's stomach clinched with sickening apprehension. His eyes swept the stateroom, and he tensed. "George, is that blood all over everything."

Marlowe dropped his head, his face working oddly. He was naked except for a pair of shorts. Farley saw that they too were smeared with red. "She's in the head," Marlowe said, softly.

Farley strode across the room, flung open the door to the adjoining head, and stared at what lay in the tub. Suddenly he turned and was extremely sick in the commode.

Marlowe came in. "I — I got carried away, Lloyd. I mean — well, it's something I've always wanted to do. I — I didn't know the little trick would bleed to death."

Farley's voice was strangled. "What did you expect? My God, George, do you know what you've done?" He whirled and was sick again.

"It can be squared," Marlowe said defiantly. "It can be squared, can't it, Lloyd?"

Farley raised his head and looked at him incredulously. "Squared? How? You — you take a girl and you..." His voice choked. "How did you expect to cut them off like that — and cut her there — and not have her bleed to death?"

"I don't know, Lloyd. I just, hell, you know how it is. I just got carried away."

Farley stared at him. Marlowe was in a cold funk, the aftermath of whiskey and a sexual orgy. Now he was up against hard reality, and he was scared silly. All at once Farley felt that knot of apprehension release itself in him. No matter what the adversity, there was always a chance for a clever man to come out on top.

"You've committed murder, George," he said coldly. "The vilest kind of murder. No matter that it is a native girl. You'll still be hanged. They hang people out here, you know."

Marlowe's lips trembled. His eyes were slimy with fear, and he put a hand on Farley's arm. "You've got to get me out of it, Lloyd. You've got to help me cover this up!"

"Help you?" Farley said coldly. "How could I help you?"

"I don't know." Marlowe drew a bloodstained hand across his eyes. "I — But there must be some way."

Farley coolly lit a cigarette, admiring the steadiness of his own hand. He was full of self-confidence again, brimming with admiration at the scheme that had presented itself to him.

"All I have to do," Farley said chillingly, "is to call in Captain Watts. Captain Watts is a New England puritan, George. No matter who he was, Watts would see the man hang who did this."

"Damnit, Lloyd —"

"But there might be a way out, George. There just might be a way out."

Marlowe let out a long breath. "Thank God. I knew you'd know a way. What is it, Lloyd?"

Farley walked out of the head and carefully selected a chair in the stateroom on which there was no blood.

"First," he said, "There are terms to discuss."

Marlowe was shaking all over. "You name them, Lloyd. Anything. I'll do anything you say."

"Including building the resort as planned?"

"Yes, of course."

"And signing over all your interest in it to me?"

Marlowe stared at him. Farley stared back, his eyes utterly without mercy. Marlowe read in them Farley's determination to have what he asked, and Marlowe let out a whistling breath.

"Yes," he said.

Farley grinned. "All right. Fine."

Marlowe reached out to touch Farley's knee. "What can you do, Lloyd?"

Farley drew back his knee quickly. "Don't get blood on these whites, George." He crushed out his cigarette in an ash tray. "Listen," he said, "we don't have much time in which to work. Carlson is on this ship, but Halu's gone back to the island. I've knocked Carlson full of dope, so he won't be awake for a long time, and even if he does wake up, he's tied to a bunk and gagged so that he can't make any trouble."

"Yes?" Marlowe waited, his face like a panful of rising dough.

"I'm going to take a small boat to shore. It'll be loaded with gin. There'll be enough to keep those islander drunk for a week. While I'm gone, you're going to have to do the same thing to Carlson that you did to her." He gestured toward the bathroom. "Whatever you used on her, use it on Carlson, too."

Marlowe stared, started to protest. Farley raised a hand.

"Only worse," Farley went on.

"But, I —"

"You've got to go back over them with the razor. Make it look like sharks did it. You ever see what a shark does, George? It just doesn't slash, it carves out great big hunks." He went on swiftly, crisply: "I'll get the islanders so drunk that when you bring two bodies ashore tomorrow and say that they were slashed by sharks, they'll be too groggy to question it. Before they sober up, we'll have the bodies disposed of in whatever fashion they use. I think they take them out to sea and roll them in. When they sober up, they'll have only the foggiest notion of what happened, and you'll be clear with them. That'll leave us free to negotiate with them after the typhoon is over and we come back."

"Yes, but —"

"But what about Captain Watts and the sailors? You'll have to sneak the bodies over the side. Don't leave any blood trail. Carry them up in blankets. Tomorrow morning, at daylight, they'll be found floating alongside. It'll look like Carlson and his wife went for a moonlight swim without a shark guard and the sharks got 'em. Then you and the crew can gather the bodies in and bring them to the island." His eyes hardened. "A tigar shark hacks up a body good," he said. "You'll have to do the same, George. Then put them over just before sunrise and as soon as the sun comes up, discover them."

"But—but I can't carry two bodies up and dump 'em by myself."

"Of course not. You'll have to have help. And there are only two people on this ship as rotten as you, George, who'd be willing to help you."

Marlowe stared at him. "Joyce and Anne?"

"That's right."

"No!" Marlowe blurted. "Those two witches — I know 'em! They'd hold it over my head the rest of my life!"

"I intend to, also," said Farley coolly. "Two more won't make any difference."

"It's fantastic. It won't work."

"It's not any more fantastic than what you've already done to her," Farley said cruelly. "And if it doesn't work, they'll hang you somewhere out here, George."

Marlowe's shoulders slumped. "All right. I'll do it. What cabin's Carlson in?"

"Number four," said Farley. "Carve him up good. Then you and Joyce and Anne sneak the bodies over just before daybreak. Retrieve them and bring them to the island. The islanders will be so drunk they'll never question the story. Carlson and his opposition to the plan will be out of the way. I'm sure Halu's hooked on gin and white women. Give him some more gin and he'll drown his grief and never suspect a thing."

"All right," Marlowe said again. "I'll do it the way you say."

"Good." Farley stood up. "Now, I'm taking the boat ashore. We have to work on a tight schedule, George. We'll have a typhoon in our lap tomorrow night." He rubbed his hands together, his eyes like garnets, hard and red in the light of the stateroom's gimbal lamp. He had known from the moment he had realized that Marlowe was brutalizing Carlson's wife that Carlson would have to die. But he had been afraid he would have to kill Carlson himself. Now it was all out of his hands. Marlowe had to do the dirty work — and he, Farley, would reap the benefits.

Margo Neal stepped out of the shower and looked at her nude body in the mirror on the back of the door. It seemed more radiant, more alive, than she seen it in a long time, and she knew why that was. Carlson. Humming softly, she turned away from the door and found a tight-fitting white blouse which she donned without a bra, a white skirt that hugged her hips. Carlson would find Tesai, and take her away from Marlowe, back to the island. When he did, Margo intended to go too. She was not through with Carlson yet, not by a long shot. She was in love with him, and she intended to use every wile at her command to make him agree with Farley's scheme so they could be together permanently.

If Carlson didn't go absolutely insane at what Marlowe had probably done to Tesai. Margo closed her eyes and shuddered slightly, remembering some of the things she had endured at the hands of her fat, aging paramour. Well, she was nearly through with that now. She could see clearly before her the pattern of a happy life. All she had to do was to convince Carlson.

Having dressed, she ran her hands over breasts and hips for one last caressing resettlement of her clothes. Then she left the stateroom, looking for Carlson.

Probably, by this time, he was in with Marlowe. She went directly to the fat man's stateroom and was about to knock on the door when she stopped, hand still poised.

Joyce Marlowe's voice said, with a certain awed admiration, "Gee, you really cut her up good, didn't you? I'll bet that would have been a sight to watch."

Anne Marlowe laughed, and it was not a pleasant sound to hear. "Our father has tried everything, hasn't he, Joycie?" Then her tone went hard and cold, dropping in timbre, but still audible through the door. "Listen, Pops, if you expect us to help you with this crazy thing, there're gonna have to be some changes made. Joyce and I can't live on that chicken feed allowance we get. And we're tired of booting around on this yacht. There aren't enough men. That damn Captain Watts won't let the sailors come near us any more. We want to go back to the States."

"Yes," she heard George Marlowe mumble. "Yes, anything. Only you've got to help me get the bodies over the rail. I'll do anything you say if you'll help me with that."

"I don't know," Joyce said tauntingly. "Carlson's too good-looking a man to cut up like that. Which part of him did you intend to slice off first? I might want to keep it for a souvenir..."

Margo Neal felt the inside of her belly go cold as the significance of what she was hearing sank in.

"Cabin four," Joyce was saying. "That's fairly close to topside. It'll be easy to take him out of there, but we're liable to have a little trouble with the one in here."

Margo Neal stood hesitantly, face contorted in terror and fear. Something had happened to Tesai — probably Marlowe had killed her in an excess of his warped passion. Now, to cover his tracks, he planned to kill Carlson also — and Carlson was in cabin four.

Margo turned away from the stateroom door and tiptoed back along the hall. She reached the ladder to topside and hurried up it silently.

Carlson awoke in darkness with a throbbing head. He opened his eyes painfully, as if the lids were of such thin tissue that they might tear. He tried tentatively to move, and all at once he realized he was bound hand and foot and that his mouth was gagged.

The stateroom in which he lay on a bunk was very dark. Carlson, his head whirling, tried to remember how he had come here. At last he recalled. Farley had given him a doped drink. But why? All he had wanted was to take Tesai back to the ship.

Tesai! He pulled against his bonds frantically. That was it! Margo had said that George Marlowe was a sadist. Something must have happened to Tesai...

Carlson twisted and writhed on the bunk, but it was no use. He was so tightly bound, his hands behind his back, that it was impossible to get loose.

Tesai — His brain raced, despite the fog that tried to slow it down. If they had injured Tesai, they knew that he and the islanders would never rest until they had exacted ultimate vengeance. So they would have to put him out of the way too.

There was fear in him as he struggled against the ropes in the darkness, but it was not nearly as strong as the anger and rage that dominated them. And not even the fear was for him — it was for his little bronze wife.

Damn them, if they had hurt Tesai —

He struggled until he was exhausted. Then, realizing that there was no hope, he lay back on the bunk; wide eyes staring into the darkness above him, heart pounding and head splitting, with nothing to do but wait like a trussed pig for the executioner, whoever he would be and with whatever instrument he chose.

Tekua and Carlson's other two wives, Kama and Valu, were very unhappy. Instead of preparing to move to the cave in the morning, they sat disconsolately in Carlson's hut.

"Our husband is not here," said Kama, "and our sister is not here, and I am worried."

"I, too," said Valu.

"But worst of all," said Tekua, "your father made us pour out the *gin*, and now we have no more of the magic drink. And it is something I crave very much."

"I would like more of it also," said Kama. "For when it is in you, you feel no worry nor depression. But when it dies away, one becomes very morose and depressed. Obviously, therefore, the thing to do is to always have the *gin* to drink so it never dies away in one."

"I wish I had more now," said Tekua. "Ai, I crave it strongly."

"So do I," said Valu. She giggled. "One thinks of so many things to do when there is *gin* in one. Still, my father is headman."

Tekua spat. "Your father admitted that he spent the whole day drinking the stuff and making love to the white women. But when *he* has had all *he* wants, no one else must drink or make love. It is most unfair."

"My father is a good headman," Valu said indigrantly. Even if he is unfair about the gin."

"The other people feel as I do," said Tekua. "I should like to see the white men bring us more of it. If they did, I do not think your father could stop us from drinking it."

Kama stared. "Do you mean the people would not obey my father? Why, that is unthinkable!"

"Is it? Why?"

Kama gestured. "I — Well, it just is."

Tekua spat again. "We have thought too long in the same way. The benefit of the *gin* is that it makes one think differently. It makes one's thoughts soar. Why should our thoughts be earthbound by your father's will?"

He tapped his chest. "I know one thing. Should I get my hands on another bottle of it, I'd like to see your father stop me from drinking it."

"Brave talk, Tekua," a voice said from the doorway behind his back.

Tekua whirled, to look into the stern face of Halu.

Then the younger man arose, no fear on his face. "Ai, Halu. Brave talk. Just as it was brave talk for you to order us to cease our merrymaking because you had had all you could stand. Not all of us are old and ineffectual like you. There are many more who feel as I do."

Halu narrowed his eyes. "There are many more who would disobey their headman for the sake of the white man's drink?"

"Ai," said Tekua. "There are many. There is talk now of making up another boat to go out to the white man's ship and get more gin."

"Listen," said Halu quickly. "A big wind will come tomorrow. The white man's ship will leave."

"All the more reason why we should get as much of the drink as we can before it does," Tekua snapped. "When the big winds come, we always huddle together, very much afraid. But if we had *gin*, it would drive away our fears with its magic and we would not be afraid during the typhoon."

"There will be no more *gin* on this island," Halu said, slowly and decisively. "*None.*"

"That, I think," said Tekua, "is no longer for you to decide. It is for the islanders to decide."

"I make the decisions for the island," Halu snapped.

Tekua's eyes narrowed and he held up one hand.

"Listen," he said. "Do you hear that? It is the sound of the white man's small boat. If he brings gin, we shall soon see who makes the decisions."

The rest of the islanders had heard the boat, too, and they had streamed down to the beach. Halu, Tekua, Kama, and Valu hurried along in their wake, just in time to see the boat beach itself and Farley climb ashore.

Bathed in the light of a moon beginning now to be veiled with the first tatters of clouds, he held up his hands in greetings. Then he gestured to the sailors and an awed sound of gratification went up from the islanders as they saw case after case of *gin* carried ashore.

Before any of them could move, Halu planted himself in front of both Farley and the gin and faced the crowd.

"Wait!" he said. "Wait! I have said there is to be no more drinking of the *gin*."

Tekua laughed loudly. "And with the big wind approaching to make us afraid, we are to obey you when all fear will be lost if we pour the contents of those bottles down our gullets?"

"If you drink this stuff," Halu roared, "you will be incapable of taking shelter."

"We will not need to take shelter, because we will no longer be afraid," said Tekua. He walked boldly forward. "I shall have my share, no matter what you say, old man."

Halu reached for his parang, but Tekua was too quick for him. Tekua moved with lean and sinewy grace and knocked Halu to the ground. As if it were a signal, the islanders surged forward.

"Wait!" Halu tried to bellow, and he would have

struggled to his feet, but his own people trampled over him in their rush to make sure they had a fair share of the drink they craved. Even his own daughters, Kama and Valu, disregarded him, stepped across his prone form, unable to think of anything but the fiery magic of the alcohol.

Farley had taken all this in very tensely. But as he saw Halu's opposition and the overcoming of it, he relaxed. One of the sailors came to him respectfully. "Mr. Farley, sir, shall we go back now?"

"Yes," Farley said. "You go back. But I'll stay here. I — I'll return to the ship first thing in the morning." He watched Halu get to his feet, shaken and trembling. The old headman stared at the mob of exuberant islanders, busy popping corks and taking the first greedy swigs. Then, head bowed, he turned and walked away down the island.

Farley grinned. "Well," he said aloud, as the small boat put back to sea, leaving him on the beach, "That takes care of the opposition. And now that I'm here, I might as well enjoy myself until Marlowe comes in the morning with the bodies." Aware that he was a little shaky himself, he too opened a bottle and took a long, fiery draught. As he lowered the bottle, his eyes lighted on the slender figures of Kama and Valu. *Carlson's other two wives,* he thought sardonically. *That would be what I call a good joke to celebrate the successful working out of the plans...*

Valu and Kama had disregarded the dejection of their father and were intent on getting drunk again as quickly as possible. Coolly, Farley walked up to them. "Hello," he said, and he put an arm around each, cupping a firm, bronze breast in each hand.

The two women looked up at him with wobbly smiles pleased, not offended. They said something in island dialect, and Farley got the idea that they wanted him to follow them. A few minutes later, they were sitting in Carlson's hut, the three of them quite naked, and Farley was enjoying the contact of the two warm, brown bodies pressed against him on either side.

First Kama, then Valu, presented open mouths for his kisses. Their tongues were flickering hot darts. They each threw a leg across Farley's legs, moving against him, and as he kissed one, the other would kiss him, greedily and unashamedly, so that before long two pairs of lips were playing up and down his body. Farley closed his eyes with the pleasure of it and lay back.

The girls bent over him. Swaying breasts brushed the length of him with their hard tips. The two mouths missed not an inch of his skin with their hungry lips and trailing tongues. Farley was bathed in a sensation of pure sensuality. *Hell,* he thought, *give the tourists this kind of treatment and they'll pay a thousand dollars a night.*

Suddenly he could stand it no longer. He seized one of the girls fiercely and threw her to her back and mounted her. She exploded under him, body writhing and arching, arms encircling him. Farley thought: *Why, they're so small, so perfect... No wonder Carlson likes it here...*

Then he felt one hand seized and lifted from the breast of the girl he was on and pressed down on the body of the other girl. He felt flesh around his hand, and another body wiggling under its touch. Then he was smothered in flesh as each of the two drunken sisters greedily sought her own satisfaction.

Carlson did not know how long he had lain in the darkness. It was a very long time and, for the first time in his life, he felt completely and absolutely helpless. Sooner or later the executioner would come. And when he did, Carlson would be at his mercy like a pig awaiting slaughter.

Who would it be? Carlson wondered. *Farley? Marlowe?*

He closed his eyes. Only when death was near did one really savor the sweetness of life. Margo ... take that interlude with her, for instance. It had been the finest thing that had ever happened to him. No matter what she was, no matter what she had been, he had to admit to himself that he was in love with her. And to keep her, he would even have yielded to her demands. He would have persuaded Halu to let Farley and Marlowe carry out their scheme.

And he would have been a fool to have done so. For there was no chance that Margo really returned his love. She was a tool of the two white men, nothing more. Undoubtedly she had been sent to influence him thus ... but now that he was to be killed, she would have lost her concern for him completely.

Carlson could not find it in himself to hate her. She was only looking out for herself. But it would have been nice if —

He discarded the thought, hearing footsteps in the corridor outside the stateroom door.

His heart pounded, he was aware of cold sweat beading his skin. It was so ironic — he had fled tens of thousands of miles, had come all the way to the Pacific, to the island of Bora-Ka — to be murdered.

Then the door cracked open. He saw three heads limned agains the light of the corridor. The door shut again, and they were in the room with him. His rolling eyes had recognized them — the Marlowe sisters and their father.

Joyce Marlowe giggled. "Don't forget my souvenir," he heard her whisper.

"Look out," Anne said. "Don't bump into that razor."

"Be quiet, both of you," Marlowe's voice said. "Carlson?"

"I'll turn on the light," said Joyce. Her voice had a tinge of shrillness in it that was insanity. "I want to watch your technique, my illustrious father." She fumbled, and the gimbal lamp, powered by the ship's generator, suddenly glowed.

Carlson writhed as he saw Marlowe standing over him with a gleaming straight razor. He tried to yell something, but the gag choked it off.

"This," Joyce said, touching Carlson. "This first. This is my souvenir..."

Marlowe said nothing. His fat face was pasty white, beaded with sweat. His hand was trembling.

"Go ahead," Anne said, the same tinge of insanity in her voice that had tremoloed in that of her sister. "Go ahead, so we can see it."

Marlowe nodded and licked his lips. He poised the razor over Carlson's throat. Carlson heard his whisper, "It'll all work out. Farley said it would." He lowered the razor until the edge of it rested like an icy hair against Carlson's throat, and Carlson, feeling as if all functions of his helpless body had already ceased, closed his eyes.

There was, at that instant, the bang of a door. A harsh voice rapped out: "Stand fast, Mr. Marlowe. If you put pressure on that, I'll have to shoot you."

Carlson's eyes flew open. As Marlowe whirled, lifting the razor, Carlson rolled on the bed.

Standing in the doorway, he saw first of all, Margo. Her eyes were enormous, her face pale. Beside her was the yacht's captain, a revolver in his hand, its muzzle trained on Marlowe's heaving belly.

Marlowe's voice trembled, partly bluster, partly fear. "Don't be an idiot, Watts. Hell, man, don't you know who I am? I'm the owner of this ship."

Watts's face was like iron, and his voice was full of scathing contempt. "You may be the owner, but you're also a murderer once and an attempted murderer again. I saw what you did to that poor native girl. And by Heaven, I'll see you hang for it. As your employee, I've stood for a lot of things, Mr. Marlowe. I've shut my eyes to vice and immorality and corruption on this ship beyond belief. But I can't shut my eyes to what Miss Neal showed me in the bath tub in your stateroom." He jerked the muzzle of the gun. "Drop the razor, Mr. Marlowe."

Marlowe stared at him for a moment. His lips moved soundlessly. Then, instead of dropping the razor, he lunged forward, flailing the blade like a lethal windmill.

The roar of the gun was tremendous in the confines of the stateroom. The impact of the bullet knocked Marlowe backward. He sank to his knees, the razor clattering to the floor, his hands over his paunch, an expression of astonishment on his face. He tried to say something then he fell forward and died.

Joyce Marlowe's insane treble broke the silence.

"The old louse had it coming to him," she giggled.

Watts's voice was like the clang of iron. "I shouldn't think you'd find it so funny, Miss Marlowe. You and your sister will be standing trial as accessories, along with Mr. Farley. Miss Neal, take that razor if you please and cut Mr. Carlson's ropes."

Margo gingerly bent and picked up the razor. But she used it deftly, and in a moment Carlson was sitting on the edge of the bed, rubbing wrists and ankles.

Margo Neal threw her arms about Carlson, flattened her breasts against him, put her cheek against his. "Oh, darling. It was such a close thing."

"You can thank Miss Neal for getting me here in time," Watts said.

Carlson held her tightly against him, savoring the warmth and life of her. He said softly: "Tesai's dead?"

"Marlowe killed her in a drunken orgy," Watts said. "I'm sorry, Mr. Carlson."

Margo pressed herself even more tightly against Carlson. "I'll make it up to you," she whispered. "Believe me, I will..."

12

THE LANCING FINGERS OF DAWN RAYED
through the hut and awoke Farley. Outside,
the wind was brisk and gray clouds scudded
across the sky. He untangled himself from
the warm and interlocked pile of flesh that was the bodies
of the two women and crawled to the front of the hut.
Stiffly, more than a little hung over with too much drink
and too much sex, he got to his feet and stepped out
into the street.

The wind was driving sand ahead of it in galloping

swirls up and down the beach, and the fronds of the palms overhead were clashing wildly. The sea had lost its placidity; huge, foaming whitecaps skirled in across the beach. The yacht bucked and pitched at anchor, far out.

Farley shaded his eyes with his hand. Damnit, where was Marlowe? He should be bringing in the two shark-ripped bodies — in a manner of speaking — by now. Farley walked down the street, peering into each hut. The all night riotous orgy that had followed his gift of the gin was still going on. The islanders were, to a man — hell, he thought, even to a child — blind drunk. When the bodies were brought in, they would pay scant attention.

Everything was in readiness, everything was fine. Except where was Marlowe and the corpses?

Then Farley saw another figure coming toward him from the end of the street. Hunched against the driving sand, he recognized Halu.

The headman was entering each hut and shouting something. Undoubtedly exhorting the islanders to sober up, Farley thought with a sardonic grin. But he wasn't having much luck. Halu was finished as headman of the island. Gin was the headman now. Gin and love. . .

It was too bad about Halu and Carlson, but there always had to be a winner and a loser. Farley had never been a winner before, and the sensation was a new and delightful one.

Farley and Halu met face to face in the center of the street and they stared one another in the eyes. If ever Farley had seen a broken man, Halu was it. His eyes were veined with the dissipation of the previous day. His shoulders were slumped in discouragement. He said something to Farley in the dialect. Farley caught both the hatred and the admission of helplessness.

Farley grinned. "Hell, chief," he said, "I know what you need." He stepped into the nearest hut, came out with a bottle of gin, thrust it at Halu. Halu stared at it and for a moment Farley thought the old man was going to knock it out of his hands. Then Farley saw Halu's tongue move across his lips. Halu made a shrug of discouragement.

"If you can't beat 'em," Farley said, "join 'em."

It was almost as if Halu understood the words. It was as if nothing mattered to Halu any longer. After a long moment, he took the bottle and uncorked it. Then he sat down crosslegged in the middle of the street, unmindful of the blowing sand, and drank deeply. Farley knew that if only Marlowe had done what he was supposed to and carried it off successfully, the capture of the island was complete.

But, damnit, where was the boat? He walked through the biting drive of the sand to the shore. The typhoon must have approached ahead of schedule. Were they afraid to put the boat ashore in those seas? They had to do it! Soon the yacht would be standing out to sea to escape the blow. There wasn't much time left. If the boat didn't come soon, he, Farley, would be stranded on the island.

Marlowe wouldn't do that, would he? Farley though with a touch of panic.

Then a gusty breath of relief went out of him. Though the distance was great, he could see the boat being lowered. He could see figures climbing into it, and a wrapped bundle being let down. The windblast made his eyes water, and he couldn't make out who the figures were, but, of course, it had to be Marlowe.

The boat lifted and dropped from view in the choppy sea. Farley waited tensely.

Then, as it came in more closely, Farley raised himself up on tiptoes and stared incredulously. Surely that was not Marlowe in the bow. Hell no, that was Carlson!

It had all gone wrong! Suddenly Farley was full of panic. Something had happened to Marlowe! Carlson was alive and that bundle must be the body of Tesai! What would the islanders say when they saw it? What would they do to him, the white man from the yacht?

Then Farley relaxed. It could be brazened out. Hell yes, anything could be brazened out. He hadn't killed the girl. Marlowe had done that. He, Farley, was as innocent as a new-born babe. Besides, the islanders were all drunk... Too drunk to do anything, too drunk to realize even what had happened. He could talk his way out of it. Hell, think of all the things he had talked his way out of before this!

He fought down an impulse to turn and run and waited for the boat.

Carlson saw Farley waiting on the beach. He swallowed hard against the hatred that overwhelmed him, and he cradled the blanket-wrapped form of Tesai more tightly in his arms. Behind him, Margo put a hand on his shoulder, and Captain Watts said: "I'll take care of Farley, Carlson. Due process of law must be followed."

Carlson said nothing.

The boat neared the beach. At last it crunched

against sand, its engine dying. Still carrying Tesai's body, Carlson stepped out of the boat. Margo and Watts followed, as did the sailors.

Only the steersman remained in the boat, playing its engine against the power of the breakers to keep it from beaching.

Farley said in a trembling voice: "Hello, Carlson. Margo. Captain Watts." He tried to make his face curious as he looked at the blanket. "What have you got there?"

"My wife," Carlson said tautly.

Watts walked up to Farley, his hand on a holstered revolver. The wind was very strong now. The steerman called: "Cap'n, you better hurry!"

"Come along, Farley," Watts said coldly. "I want you in the boat. Marlowe's dead. You and his daughters will stand trial as accessories to murder."

Farley gave a shuddering laugh. "Why, Captain, you must be out of your mind. I don't know anything about a murder."

"The Marlowe girls tell a different story," Watts said. He unsnapped the flap of his holster. "You'll get your chance in court. You're damned lucky I'm not trying you at sea."

"Captain, I —" And suddenly Farley saw it all looming ahead of him. The prison, the end of dreams, the complete finality of knowing that he would never strike it rich. He saw himself as he really was, a two-bit drifter who would stop at nothing, a man incapable of being as smart as he thought he was. The picture was a sickening one, a sobering one.

Panic rose within Farley. He could not bear the

thought of being shut away. To never know the thrill of trying to outwit a new sucker; to never touch a woman's body, to cease to live, only to exist; a thwarted animal in a cage, a victim of his own cleverness.

"Cap'n, these breakers are too much!" The steersman yelled. "You'd better hurry."

Suddenly Farley made his break. He did it blindly not knowing why nor where he would go. But if he could just reach the yacht, there was a chance it would have to sail before the others would rejoin it. He knew the mate, he was a sucker. If the yacht had to leave Watts until the typhoon was over, there was a chance that he could outwit the mate, make it to safety somewhere...

It was a wild chance, a crazy one, but Farley had never been able to figure chances rationally. Suddenly he ran.

He ran into the surf and leaped into the boat. The steersman, caught by surprise, gave a startled yell as Farley seized him and threw him overboard. Then Farley had gunned the engine and, as a pistol bullet sang by his head, almost indistinguishable from the sound of the wind, he was swinging the boat around and out to sea.

"Damnit!" Watts yelled. "We'll be stranded here! The mate had orders to put to sea no later than a half hour from now." He fired at Farley again.

But Farley was making distance now, between the island and the boat. The boat humped and shook itself as it crested the waves, truly giant-size now, that boomed in across the reef. Farley laughed in triumph. One thing he knew was how to handle a boat. He'd learned that in the long ago, as a child growing up on Key West. He had left Watts behind. No more small boats would be able to travel through the surf in this freshening wind. He would throw himself on the mercy of the mate on the yacht, somehow bribe or con the mate —

A huge sea rose in front of him, its top beginning to froth with white. Farley gunned up it, then cut power as the boat slipped into the trough.

Then he stared incredulously. Out there, between himself and the yacht, a wave was gathering itself. Hundreds, perhaps thousands of footpounds of wind picked it up and drove it along. Compared to a genuine typhoon wave, it was nothing, just a harbinger of what was to come. But for a man in a small boat, it was looming disaster.

Farley held his breath and waited for the precise moment to give the craft power as the wave pounded toward him. It was a wall of water fifteen feet high. He watched in amazement as it built itself higher, looming twenty feet now. Hell! The boat might swamp!

It was now or never. Farley gunned the engine. He and the crest of water charged at each other. Farley saw tht green tower above him, waiting to drop and smash him. The boat climbed, stalled, its propeller bit and it climbed again.

But not enough. The wall of water, tons of it, filled the boat and turned it over and threw it back toward shore like a chip. Farley was not in it.

He was deep beneath the surface. His eyes were blinded by his own swirling hair. His nose and mouth and lungs were full of water. He was drowning; tossing and turning and bobbing as he sank, his arms powerless against the mighty strength of the ocean.

And at last he quit fighting and let himself sink.

Always a loser, he thought despairingly.

If only. . ., he thought, and then he quit thinking, forever.

Inside the cave, it was very dark. It was dark outside now, too. The typhoon was roaring with full force across the island, torrents of rain driven vertically across the face of the islanders' traditional place of refuge.

Within the cave, the people of Bora-Ka sat in silence, families huddled together, each one of them deep in inner gratitude that they were not out in this, the fiercest storm any of them had seen.

But they would have been. They would have been caught in a drunken stupor if it had not been for the body of Tesai.

Carlson had unrolled the blanket on the ground. "Come," he had yelled angrily. "Come and see what the white man's way does. Come and see the abomination we have all allowed to be committed in our lust for *gin!*"

And the islanders, drunky and groggy, had come at last as the word had spread.

And one by one, as they had viewed in horror the body of Tesai, horribly mutilated, slashed and breastless, the islanders had sobered.

"Is this the white man's way?" Tekua had asked sickly, incredulously.

"It is the way of those who drink beyond rationality and lust beyond reason," Carlson told them harshly.

The islanders stared at one another. The idea of committing such torture on the body of another human being was incredible to them, shattering.

"Would we do things like that if we continue to

drink the white man's drink?" Tekua whispered.

"Ai," answered Kama, weeping softly. "Because it is not our drink. Our bodies and our minds are not accustomed to it. Our father told us. Last night he told us, but we would not listen. Oh, my father!" She flung her arms around Halu's neck.

He disengaged them gently. "There is no time for grief!" he roared. "The storm grows worse. Everyone to the cave!"

Again his voice had the headman's authority. The people of Bora-Ka did not hesitate, but obeyed immediately.

Now Carlson, far back in the cave, held Kama tightly in one arm. Valu huddled against her. Carlson's other arm was about Margo Neal.

"When the yacht comes back," Carlson said, "you and Captain Watts and the sailors can leave the island. It shouldn't be long."

"No," Margo said tonelessly. "It shouldn't be long."

Suddenly Carlson was aware that she had taken his hand and placed it over one soft breast. She squeezed his palm down into the yielding flesh, and she turned to him in the darkness of the cave. He felt the warmth of her breath on his face.

"What," she asked, "if I didn't want to go?"

Carlson could not speak for a moment. When he did answer, his voice was incredulous. "You mean stay on Bora-Ka?"

"Yes."

"But — nobody's going to carry out any scheme like Farley's or Marlowe's now There won't be any civilization here now. The chance of repetition of a typhoon like this will scare away everybody for years to come."

"I know," Margo said. Her voice trembled. "I know, and I don't care. If I can only stay here with you."

Suddenly Carlson held her tightly against him. "You don't mean that?" he said gently.

"I do mean it."

"But you don't know what it involves. The native diet, sleeping on a reed mat, a wooden pillow. And — and I still have two wives, you know. You — you would have to share me with them."

Margo took a deep breath, and he felt her breast rise beneath his palm.

"I could be number three wife," she said.

"Why?" Carlson asked fiercely. "Why do you want to be?"

"Because," she whispered, "I love you."

Carlson was silent for a moment. Then he said: "You really mean it, don't you?"

"I really mean it," Margo said desperately.

Carlson turned to Kama and Valu. "My wives," he said. "The white woman named Margo wants to stay with us. I shall marry her and bring her to join us in our hut. What do you think of the idea?"

"The white woman is very beautiful and she seems kind," said Kama.

"She could be a sister to us," said Valu, "to replace the sister we have lost."

"Our hut would be empty without a third woman," said Kama.

"We think it is a fine idea," said Valu.

Carlson turned back to Margo. "If you're really

serious," he said, "Kama and Valu think it's a fine idea."
He hesitated. "So do I. Because I happen to love you
too."

She burrowed her face against him. "When can we
be married?"

Carlson smiled in the darkness. "Any time," he
said. "Why not now?"

"Now?" Margo raised her head. "What do you
mean?"

"Among the people of Bora-Ka," said Carlson, "the
marriage ceremony is the performance of the act of love
before the whole tribe." He paused. "The whole tribe is
in this cave."

He felt the hard tips of Margo's breasts against him
through her blouse. Her voice was low and throaty.

"Then let it be now," she said.

In the darkness, Carlson fumbled for the buttons
of her blouse. She helped him. He felt the warmth of
her heavy breasts thrusting free as she shrugged out of
the fabric, and he ran his hand over the velvety skin.
She was already shrugging out of the skirt.

"I imagine," she whispered, "it's the last time I'll
wear such civilized garments. With my black hair, five
years from now, no one will be able to tell me from a
native."

"I will," Carlson said, and he found her body in the
dark. His mouth dropped to her breasts, and she surged
upward against him hungrily.

Kama and Valu watched as best they could in the
darkness. "Now," Valu said, "everything will be as it was
before. We will have a new sister and there will be three

of us in the hut."

"No," Kama said thoughtfully, "nothing will be as it was before. The things we have learned, we cannot erase. If we make them shameful, they will be practiced in secret and we shall feel guilty. If they are declared taboo, there will be those who will break the taboo. Though we have thrown the *gin* away, we shall remember that, too. We shall yearn for it for a long time, and when we can get it, some of us will. The trader will bring new things for us when he comes, and we will have to work harder to pay him for them. No, much has been brought to his island and too little taken away. I am not sure things will be as they were at all."

"We shall see," said Valu, and she held her sister's hand. While their husband took his third wife, they sat together in the darkness and looked out the cave at the driving rain and gusting wind that, together, were doing their best to sweep the island clean.